CHARLOTTE LAMB

night music

Harlequin Books

TORONTO • LONDON • LOS ANGELES • AMSTERDAM
SYDNEY • HAMBURG • PARIS • STOCKHOLM • ATHENS • TOKYO

Harlequin Presents edition published January 1981
ISBN 0-373-10404-9

Original hardcover edition published in 1980
by Mills & Boon Limited

CHAPTER ONE

LISA looked into the filing cabinet and sighed. She had been away for a week, and during her absence Joan Brown had taken over her work. Joan disliked filing, and disposed of letters in a very simple fashion; either by flinging them all helter-skelter into the Miscellaneous section, or by stuffing them guiltily behind the nearest large object in the hope that no one would notice their failure to appear in the correct file.

It often amused Lisa that perfectly capable, sensible people like Joan should have these odd blind spots. Joan's other work was quite efficient. It was only when faced with filing that she became frantic. Perhaps she needed some outlet for hidden dislike of order.

She was talking now behind Lisa, leaning against the desk, her arms folded, giving Lisa a breakdown on all the events in the office during the last week. Having finished this, she paused and then said, 'So, you had a good time?'

'Very.' Lisa had begun to realise how much she would have to do this morning. Before she could launch into the usual routine she would have to prowl around and investigate the results of Joan's temporary reign in the office. She pulled out a crumpled letter from behind the Busy Lizzie pot plant and smoothed it out. Joan looked at her with innocent eyes. Lisa did not say a word, merely scanned the letter and then filed it.

The door opened and Joan hurriedly stopped talking, straightened up and vanished through the side door into the typing pool.

'My God, thank heavens you're back!' Jon Lister put both hands to his head. 'Another day and I'd have strangled her! She managed to lose a vital letter from Compton and of course Evan suddenly demanded it. He blamed me and when I asked her where it was she just looked at me like an idiot and said: "What letter?" Then when I shouted she burst into tears.'

'You shouted?' Lisa smiled at him. 'I don't believe it.'

'Neither did I at the time,' he said with self-deprecatory wryness. 'But even I have my limits, and that girl is one.' His blue eyes ran over her with a look of surprise. 'Every time I see you I think I must be imagining things. I kept looking at her and thinking that I could be looking at you, and then I wanted to drop a wastepaper basket over her head.'

She laughed and her eyes were affectionate. Jon had a gentleness which she found very appealing, a steady quietness, unmarred by any tendency to grab, which she appreciated.

He paused now and said soberly, 'I've missed you.'

Lisa did not answer that, only smiled again. Much as she liked him she did not want him to get the wrong impression. There was no future in their relationship.

He looked away and asked: 'Good holiday?'

'Very,' she said, as she had said to Joan. 'How is the Pickton account?'

His mouth turned down at once and her heart sank. 'Pickton wasn't exactly overjoyed,' Jon told her, shrugging.

She sighed. 'I'm sorry.' The trouble was that Jon was in the wrong business. He was a methodical, hard-working man, but he had no flair. He had got this job only because his brother-in-law happened to be the managing director, but Evan Wright would not put up with losing accounts through mishandling. Jon did just well enough to put a gloss on things, but every time he made a mistake, Evan's eyes grew colder and his temper more hair-trigger. The situation was causing rows between Evan and his wife Anna, Jon's sister. Anna was a devoted sister. Jon was six years her junior and she would fight to the death for him, if she had to, which was admirable. It was unfortunate that the man she was fighting at the moment happened to be her husband.

If the firm whose account he was handling happened to be a long established and conservative firm, all was well. Jon was happy following a precedent and he made a dutiful employee. If he got a more adventurous and demanding client, Jon was in deep water. His brain was too slow to come up with novel ideas. Quick-talking company men terrified him.

'What did you do on holiday?' Jon asked, breaking into her thoughts.

'Sunbathed.' She smiled at him. 'What more could anyone want on holiday?'

'You're certainly an advertisement for it,' Jon replied, smiling back. 'You've come back with quite a tan.'

'I had the start of one before I left,' she reminded him. 'I'm lucky I tan at all. With my skin I ought to go scarlet and then peel.' Her natural skin tones were pale and fine, but she had learnt to use lotion to acclimatise her skin to a hotter sun and now she was glowing golden brown, her throat and shoulders bared in her dress, gleaming like oiled silk. The burnished tangles of her copper-coloured hair hung down her back, brushed into full soft coils around her face, thick and cloudy and glinting in the sunlight. The smooth tanned skin threw her green eyes into prominence, deepening their colour. Lisa felt herself very lucky to have inherited from her parents a combination of health and looks which had made life enjoyable, but some of the reactions her looks received from the men had lately begun to irritate her.

Although her face was beautiful, it was her long supple, swaying body men stared at with riveted attention. Once that had not bothered her, but her feelings had changed suddenly, leaving her with a residue of hostility towards a certain sort of man. She was sick of men who couldn't keep their hands to themselves. It was Jon's restraint in that direction that had made him acceptable to her. Jon kept his hands to himself, and that suited Lisa.

'What else did you do on holiday?' Jon asked.

'Nothing.' She laughed, seeing his disgusted look. 'I just lay on the beach all day and soaked up the sun.' Shrugging, she added, 'That's why I went to Spain—the sun, and the lazy atmosphere.'

'You didn't do any sightseeing?' Jon took his holidays as seriously as he took the rest of his life. He would have assiduously investigated the surrounding district if he had been with Lisa. She laughed at him without real annoyance.

'I did what I went there to do. Nothing.'

'You should have gone to Italy,' said Jon, looking wistful. 'There's such a lot to see over there. I've been twice and I still never get time to see half the things I want to see. It seems a waste of a holiday to spend it lying on the beach.'

'You have your fun, I'll have mine,' Lisa told him firmly. She adored lying in the sun, feeling the heat soak into her grateful skin, the sound of the sea just a few yards away and the faintest of breezes rippling through a beach umbrella over her head. That was her idea of heaven. She was the sort of girl who worked hard and efficiently when she was at work. When she was on holiday she did nothing at all.

She had gone on holiday with her flatmate, Magda, who worked in the art department. Within weeks of Lisa's arrival at Wrights, the two girls had become friendly. It was Magda who had suggested that they share a flat. She had been wryly frank. 'Sharing with you could be a boon. You're bound to get more offers than you can cope with, and I might get the fallout.'

Lisa had laughed, her green eyes amused but half

angry. 'Come off it! You don't have any trouble finding your own men.'

'I'm not in your league, baby.' Magda was a slim, shapely girl with curly dark hair and a wide smile, but although she was attractive she envied Lisa her rather more dramatic effect on the men in the office.

'You can get very sick of it,' Lisa had warned her, and Magda had sighed.

'Not me,' she had claimed. 'I'd never get tired of having all those heads turn.'

'It's not the heads you have to worry about,' Lisa had commented drily.

Jon perched on her desk and watched her filing the last of the hidden letters she had discovered during her search of the office. The door behind them was flung open suddenly. Evan Wright roared into the room—Evan never went anywhere quietly. 'God Almighty!' he bellowed, and then stopped dead as he caught sight of Lisa.

Evan adored his wife and had never been known to be even remotely interested in any other woman, but as his appreciative eyes wandered from Lisa's bright hair to her gleaming golden shoulders and down the long-limbed, supple body, she saw a gleam come into his round yellow eyes.

'Hallo, I'd forgotten you were due back today. You look fantastic.' His admiration was automatic and unaggressive. He always registered her looks, sighed and shrugged them away. Evan was strictly a one-woman man.

With the sudden switching-off which demonstrated his ability to concentrate on what mattered at the moment, he swung back at once to his brother-in-law with a baring of teeth.

'You stupid bastard, do you ever listen? How many times must I tell you that Renton has a hang-up about sex? Why did you put up that artwork? For the last time, keep girls out of the Renton account. I've had him on the phone for the last ten minutes screaming like a constipated frog.' He turned to Lisa, rumpling his short, thick hair. 'Hell, Lisa, keep him out of trouble, will you? I might get mad enough to sack him, and then Anna will probably divorce me.'

He blew out of the room without waiting for an answer from either of them. Jon had learnt, in any case, never to answer back. Evan's energy and drive made him a formidable opponent in an argument. Jon always lost. Faced with his brother-in-law's aggression, he curled up into a shivering ball and hid.

Now he groped his way into his own office, his face averted from her, and she sighed. Poor Jon! If he had any sense he would get out of this job and find one which could use the talents he did have— his care and method, his passion for routine, his level temperament. Those were gifts which were useless to him in this job. As Evan often shouted at him, what they needed were ideas. 'Ideas! Know what I mean? Ever had any? Or is that head of yours full of air?'

Evan despised Jon for what he was because what Evan wanted him to be was someone with an intuitive grasp of the work; someone whose brain spawned fresh approaches, someone quick and witty, shrewd and imaginative. Someone, in fact, like Evan himself.

It was so easy for a man like Evan, who took life by the throat and shook it into obedience, to look down on someone like Jon who was capable of nothing of the kind.

The telephone rang and Lisa dealt with a query, then got on with her morning routine. When she first applied for this job, Evan had looked at her with narrowed eyes and asked if she had ever thought of modelling. 'You'd be a sensation,' he had told her. 'Want me to fix it for you?' Lisa had refused coolly. It had amazed Evan, who had apparently expected her to jump at the chance. She had no intention of explaining her reasons and Evan had decided she was just lacking in ambition.

Judging her on her looks, he had not expected her to be very bright or efficient, but he had put her with Jon on the theory that she might distract and propitiate infuriated clients even if she couldn't do the work too well. But Lisa had astonished Evan with her grasp of the job and her hard-working efficiency. She had not cared to explain to him that she worked hard because she was proving something to herself. She had changed her whole life when she came to England and the way she did her job had been a deliberate part of that.

Jon poked his head round the door later that afternoon to ask if he could take her out to dinner. She accepted, merely to see a smile come back into his tired face. He had spent the day beating his brains out over the Renton account. He did try. It was a pity there were no prizes for trying in that business. Advertising was a tough game. Winners got all the glory; losers got nothing but glum looks.

'What on earth do you see in Jon?' Magda asked her that evening. She was lounging on Lisa's bed, watching her slide into the smooth dark green dress she was going to wear for her date with Jon.

Lisa shrugged. 'I like him. Zip me up, will you?'

Magda obliged, looking over Lisa's bare shoulder, eyeing her reflection and ruefully registering the oval face from which wide green eyes stared back at her, their darkened lashes thick and long. Lisa had a rounded chin with a faint cleft, a classically straight nose and a mouth which only just missed being too wide. It was the facial feature she had once most worried about, fretting because she fancied it marred her looks, but it was also the feature men stared at with most interest. The full, passionate lower lip promised a sensuous response which matched the swaying curves of her body.

'I just don't get it,' Magda commented. 'Why Jon? He's such a rabbit.'

'Maybe I like rabbits.' Jon suited her because he was no problem. She never had to fight off wandering hands or lose her temper with him. He was quiet and gentle and easily held at a distance. The only feeling Jon aroused in her was pity. Lisa had no wish to feel anything for anyone; she had had enough of feelings to last her a lifetime.

'Are you frigid?' Magda asked with her customary bluntness.

Lisa laughed, something in the darting green flash

of her eyes making Magda laugh too. 'No, just careful,' she assured her.

Magda considered that, watching her as she checked over her appearance.

'I suppose you must have had to fight men off for years. I wish I could have your problem for a day or two!'

'That's about how long it would take you to get thoroughly sick of it,' Lisa told her flatly. 'Believe me, it's no fun. For every man whose interest you welcome, there are a hundred who make you want to scream.' It had taken her some time to realise that the way she looked gave men the wrong impression of her. At first she had been baffled at having to fight off permanent approaches of a certain sort. Many of the girls she had worked with had been happy with the situation. They got both fun and profit out of it. Lisa had been too serious-minded. She hadn't been looking for a mink coat and a handsomely furnished flat. She had never put into words just what she was looking for—but it had not ever been offered to her by any of the men she dated.

'You're very secretive,' Magda complained. 'Hasn't there ever been anyone special?'

Lisa's face was determinedly blank. 'Everyone thinks he's special,' she said evasively, turning away.

Jon arrived exactly at the time he had promised. He smiled and said a few polite words to Magda, who rather obviously had to repress a desire to yawn. Although Jon was by no means bad looking, Magda had no time for him. 'He bores me stiff,' she had told Lisa, and her manner now made no attempt to hide that fact.

As they drove away a few moments later, Jon looked recklessly at Lisa. 'We're going to celebrate.'

'We are? What?' She was taken by surprise, her green eyes opening wide as she stared at him.

'Nothing,' said Jon. 'Anything. I'm sick of being gloomy.'

She laughed and looked at him with the compassionate fondness which was her strongest feeling towards him. He made her feel maternal. He had the same effect on his sister and possibly on a lot of other women. The female sex was divided generally into two halves where Jon was concerned—those who worried over him and those who despised him.

'What a brilliant idea,' Lisa told him. 'Who says you've got no flair? Let's celebrate by all means. All we have to do is think of a reason.'

'Your first day back at work,' said Jon, looking sideways. 'That's worth celebrating.'

He spoke without undue emphasis, as he always did. His manner, in fact, determined the impact he made. The soft, tentative tone of his voice, the hesitancy with which he often spoke, his lack of drive and permanent air of apology, made him somehow a shadow of what he might have been if his nature had been different. Jon was a tall, slim man with light fair hair and pale blue eyes, his features regular and quite attractive in a good mood.

He had a low sex drive; a fact of which Lisa was perfectly aware. It suited her. Just occasionally she

wondered if Jon had ever felt passion, but she had
no intention of finding out. You never knew what
manner of genie you were letting out of the bottle
when you tampered with a man's ego. She did not
want Jon to alter in that respect.

'Where are we going?' she asked, watching him as
he nervously fielded an attack by a low-slung sports
car endeavouring to force him out of its path so that
it could zoom ahead.

'I managed to get a table at Ferrelli's.' He looked
at her with a complacent expression. It was hard to
get a table at one of the most exclusive restaurants
in town. Ferrelli's had a reputation for ruthless screen-
ing of customers. If your name was not on their list of
desirable people, they blandly told you they were full
up. You did not just walk in off the street. You had
a reservation, and to get one you had to have a
reference or a recognised name.

'How did you manage that?' she asked with an
amazed face. In fact, she had already guessed. One of
the other executives had recently handled the Ferrelli account when they opened up in the States.
Jon would have been able to pull strings. It was
lucky, she mused, that he hadn't handled the account himself or they would never have got a table.

Jon took some time in explaining it to her. He had
a habit of laying out his conversation like a railway
line before he actually got to the real point which one
could see coming a mile off, but which one couldn't
halt without hurting his feelings. Jon would merely
be thrown right off balance if one interrupted.

She smiled as she listened, watching him, her eyes

rueful. It was a relief to be with him after some of her experiences in the past. Jon liked going out with her for two reasons, and Lisa was aware of both of them. He was delighted by the envious looks he got from other men. It boosted his ego to be seen with her. Also he found her uncritical acceptance of him soothing. Other girls found his slow voice and careful patterns of behaviour irritating.

They were both of them in flight from reality, Lisa thought. She wondered if Jon ever thought about her motives for dating him, and doubted it. He acted as a shield for her, keeping other men away, glossing over her hidden hostility towards his sex. To Jon she was a trophy which improved his image both to himself and to the other men in the office.

Evan had bluntly commented on their dates. 'You screwy? He's as dull as ditchwater. Couldn't you find something more interesting?'

She had gazed at him coolly. 'I'm quite happy, thank you.'

Evan's yellow eyes had probed her face. 'Funny girl.' He was curious about her and made no attempt to hide it. Her looks should have made her ambitious in one way or another. Evan found it intriguing that they apparently had had the opposite effect. Lisa had resisted all his attempts to get her to talk about her past. To Evan she was a mystery he was dying to uncover.

Ferrelli's was a discreetly hidden-away building in the heart of Mayfair. When they had parked, with great difficulty, they walked to it along quiet streets which in the daytime were crowded with cars and

people. Ferrelli's was crowded when they walked into
it, but it didn't show. The secret of the appeal of the
place was that they managed somehow to give a
private, intimate feel to the spacing of the tables, the
soft roseate light lowered around each to enclose
them in a world of their own, excluding everyone
but the soft-footed, silent waiters who came and
went along the room.

The head waiter glanced at Jon, his left brow
writhing upward in disbelief. Jon was immaculately
dressed, but she guessed that from tonight he would
never again get a table here. His faint stammer, his
air of apology, spoke for him. The man smiled
politely, bending that black head which had a boot-
polish gleam to the smoothed-down hair. As he
straightened his eyes slid to Lisa and a very different
look came into them. His narrowed, thoughtful gaze
told her that he had the feeling he had seen her before but could not recall where. Part of his stock in
trade was undoubtedly his incredible memory for
faces and names. He relied on it to test the clientele
as they arrived.

As they followed him through the shadowy passage between tables, the man kept glancing at her,
his brows still furrowed. Lisa kept her face blank.
Jon was looking around him with a tense face, his
hand at his tie, feeling too obviously out of place and
ill at ease.

There were famous faces at some of the tables.
Jon saw them and gulped. Lisa sighed. She slid her
hand through his arm, smiling sideways with a flick

of her lashes, willing him to stop looking like a man going to his execution.

Suddenly she felt a strange frisson run down her spine. Her copper head lifted and she had to repress a desire to turn and see who was watching her. Someone was, she knew that. She fought down an urge to look round. It was probably merely some man with wandering eyes.

The head waiter held her chair and deftly slid it forward as she sat down. Bending, he murmured softly: 'Would Madame care to choose an aperitif?'

She smiled at Jon across the table. 'What shall I have, darling?'

The head waiter took on a faint glint of amusement, unfooled by her pretty air of submission. Jon mumbled, thrown by the question, and the man suggested a few drinks. Jon seized on one and the man took two menus from a hovering waiter and handed them with a bow to first Lisa and then Jon. After that he vanished into the shadows while they studied the menu.

The drinks arrived. She sipped hers while Jon huskily gave their order to the waiter. She could still feel those eyes watching her and now she could look without being obvious since she was seated facing the direction from which she sensed the stare came.

She did not hurry. Leaning across the table, she touched Jon's hand. 'What do you think of Ferrelli's?'

'Fantastic,' Jon said unhappily. He sounded as if

he couldn't wait to get out of the place. He hated
risking snubs and he was laying himself open to one
by being so nervous. She saw him glance miserably
at the next table where a small thin man was dining
with a statuesque lady in a very simple dress
stamped Paris and a string of matching pearls which
were not cultured. Jon looked down at his drink, and
she could read his mind. He was wishing himself a
million miles from here. The suit he was wearing was
his best and the head waiter had priced it at a glance.
Some of the customers dining here tonight would
think nothing of paying as much for their meal.

'Cheer up,' she murmured, smiling encouragingly
at him.

As if she could see inside his head she knew that
he was thinking that he had made yet another disastrous mistake. He had brought her here to boost his
deflated ego after a bad day. Now he felt he had
merely made his life worse.

Evan made Jon feel inferior every day; Ferrelli's
was making him feel two inches high.

Lisa flicked a glance past his shoulder towards the
table from which she sensed that stare was coming.

The shadowy room seemed to dissolve like the
delusion of a nightmare. Her heart stopped and then
began again with a fast, painful rhythm.

He was very tall, his broad shoulders casually
lounging back against his chair, one hand holding a
wine glass which he twirled as he watched her. As
she met those blue eyes, a mocking smile came into
them which was not reflected in the hard, straight
mouth.

She had intended to enjoy this meal, this taste of a life she had walked out of and which she did not regret too much, but now she had only one idea in her head. She wished she had the nerve to get up and walk out.

She shuddered inwardly at the idea of eating a leisurely meal while those blue eyes travelled over her, as they were doing now; narrowed, hard, sardonic.

Out of the corner of her eye she scrutinised the woman he was seated opposite. Her hair was a fashionably styled blonde. Lisa heard the husky laughter as she gazed invitingly at her companion across the table. She was beautiful, of course; she wouldn't be dining with him if she wasn't. They made a matching pair and the blonde was welcome to him.

Jon began to enjoy himself as the wine reached his head. His face had flushed and he talked more confidently. Lisa concentrated on him, smiling at everything he said, ignoring the glances she was still getting from the other man.

Would he come over here? That was the question which was really obsessing her under the cover of her bright smiles. He was with another woman. He could hardly just walk away from the expensive-looking blonde to break into somebody's conversation. The ethics of polite society wouldn't bother him, of course—anyone looking at that arrogant face could see that. Just as Jon carried his meek conciliating nature in his face, this man carried ruthless confidence in his; in every movement he made.

Without so much as glancing in his direction Lisa was conscious of him all the time: the rake of the long hand through thick dark hair, the curl of his mouth, the shift of his legs.

He knew, of course. Across the room they were having a silent duel of which everyone else was oblivious.

Lisa stared at her wine glass and considered the ironies of fate with a wry mouth.

She had kept away from places like this with such care in the past year. If she had not been sorry for Jon she would never have accepted the invitation. Hadn't she learnt even now that pity could be as dangerous as any other emotion?

The evening had taken on something of the feel of an endurance test. Lisa ate food she never tasted and listened to talk she never heard. Jon seemed unaware of her absorption in other things and quite satisfied with her blank smiles and faint murmurs whenever he paused. He had drunk enough to be past caring. They would have to take a taxi home, she decided, at one point, eyeing his perspiring face.

When she tentatively suggested that they might leave when they had finished the meal, he looked at her in amazement. He was having the time of his life now that he had managed to distance the rest of the world with the help of sufficient wine. He called for another brandy and lit a cigar, obviously feeling on top of life.

When the other man and his companion rose, Lisa almost groaned with relief. She kept her eyes down until they had steered out of the restaurant.

He had gone. She was both dazed with relief and incredulous.

When Jon felt he had had enough of the heady pleasure of living in another world, he paid the bill with a concealed disbelief at the size of it and steered her out of the restaurant into a taxi.

She had not needed to over-persuade him that he was in no state to drive his car. Jon was always amenable, even after all that wine.

They were almost at her flat when Lisa suddenly noticed the sleek white limousine following them, and she sat forward in sudden tension, staring at it, trying to catch a glimpse of the driver. The darkness hid his face.

She was being over-imaginative, she told herself firmly. It couldn't be.

The taxi pulled up outside the house in which she and Magda had their flat. Jon kissed her with more enthusiasm than he normally betrayed, and she submitted without any enthusiasm at all; the whole of her mind occupied by the realisation that the white car had parked directly behind the taxi, and that the driver whose face she could still not see was staring at their entwined outlines.

'Goodnight, Jon,' she said, diving out of the taxi. She ran down the steps into the paved area outside her front door. The flat was in the basement of a tall house. It gave a privacy which other flats would have lacked, since not only did they have their own front door but they had a paved space outside it which they had turned into a very pretty town garden. They had bought some stone urns in which they grew geraniums and a flat stone slab seat beside which they had a rather wispy rose tree in a large pot. The flowers gave a vivid splash of colour to the drab street. Magda had painted their front door a brilliant yellow to add to the general cheerfulness.

Magda would be asleep, of course. It was past midnight. Lisa did not put on the light. She went to the window in the sitting-room and discreetly parted the curtains, peering out. She heard the heavy throb of the taxi as it turned the corner. Silence descended.

The street seemed deserted. Had she after all imagined that white car? Had it all been a coincidence?

She was about to draw the curtain again when she heard the slow click of feet on the pavement above the area.

She drew back, holding the curtain but keeping out of sight. The iron gate at the top of their steps creaked in its familiar way. A black shadow fell across the paving stones, moving slowly.

Lisa's nerves screamed. She had been expecting something of this sort ever since she set eyes on that face in Ferrelli's. She had known all the time that, having once found her again, he would not just walk away. Across that elegant, exclusive room his cynical eyes had told her that. He had raised his wine glass in a sardonic, anticipatory salute.

She wouldn't open the door, of course; she was not that much of a fool. But he knew where she was now—he had her address and no doubt he had discovered at Ferrelli's just who Jon was and uncovered the agency name. He had all the necessary pieces of information.

She looked obliquely through the curtain. He stood outside, his hands in his pockets, watching the window. He knew she was there.

He moved and she heard his voice quite distinctly, although he spoke quietly.

'Let me in, Lisa.'

She didn't answer. With trembling hands she dragged the curtains together and sank into the nearest chair, pressing her fingers into her aching eyes as though to soothe away the pain which she knew very well would not be soothed.

He gave a sharp, peremptory rap on the door, being careful not to make too much noise. He would not want to attract attention, any more than she did.

She didn't move, her head buried in her hands. Go away, she thought silently. There was a silence which somehow made her all the more nervous, then she heard the soft footsteps withdrawing, the creak of the gate again. He had decided against trying to force an entry. That did not mean he had given up, of course. He had a score he wanted to settle with her, and he was not a man who forgot unpaid bills.

She heard the soft purr of his engine and then the car drew away. She forgot the time, crouched in her chair. What now? She had been gradually learning to live a quiet life at Wrights, her days peaceful and uneventful, unmarred by anything but bitter memories, and even those had slowly been receding a little.

Aching, she got up and looked at the clock. Two in the morning! She must be crazy to be sitting here, shivering in the middle-of-the-night chill. She had to get up at seven-thirty, and she was going to feel like limp, chewed string tomorrow.

When she passed Magda's door she heard the other girl's slow, quiet breathing, and envied her that untroubled mind. The worst of Magda's problems was the spot she suspected was coming on her neck. She had spent half an hour this evening scrutinising herself in the mirror from all angles.

Stepping into her own room, Lisa hurriedly undressed and began a speeded up version of her nightly routine. She forced from her mind every thought of those blue eyes, the slow, sensual appraisal which had wandered over her body and made her pulses leap and flame in a response which maddened her.

Slipping into bed, she lay in the darkness, schooling her mind to expel him, but knowing that was impossible. There was too much between them. He would be back. She wouldn't get rid of him that easily.

Trying to be cool and sensible, she asked herself what he could do to her and then shivered away from any admission.

Why else had she run and kept on running? She knew what he could do to her all right.

The telephone began to ring. Her heart leapt. She

jumped out of bed, stubbing her toe on the bedside table. Magda stirred, her bedsprings creaking. Lisa tore out of the door and ran into the sitting-room. She was out of breath as she picked up the phone.

Somehow she gasped out the number. The line was open, she could hear quiet breathing, but nobody spoke.

'Hallo,' she said sharply, although she knew now who was on the other end and her first instinct was to slam the phone down.

'I haven't forgotten, Lisa,' a voice whispered. 'Did you think I had?'

She closed her eyes, then she slammed the phone down.

No, she had not thought he had forgotten. She stared at nothing with wide, disturbed eyes.

Magda struggled through the door, yawning widely, her small white teeth catlike. 'Who on earth was that at this hour?'

'A heavy breather,' Lisa lied.

'Why can't they do their breathing before I get to bed?' Magda covered another yawn. 'I'll be dead tomorrow.' She eyed Lisa. 'Had a good evening? Where did you go?'

'Ferrelli's.'

Magda did a double-take. 'You're kidding!'

Lisa forced a smile. 'No.'

'How did Jon get a table?'

'Personality,' said Lisa with a dry intonation.

Magda looked at her with disbelief. 'What was it like? Is the food as good as they say?'

'Fabulous.' Lisa was not really listening. She was remembering the soft purr of that voice and her skin was cold.

'What did you have?'

Lisa couldn't remember and her blank face made Magda stare even more. 'Don't tell me Jon was so fascinating you didn't notice what you were eating?'

'Terrible confession, isn't it?' Lisa laughed, wondering if she looked as scared stiff as she felt.

'I'm off to bed,' said Magda, drooping as she turned away. 'Tell me all about it in the morning. And if our heavy breather gets back to us tell him to drop dead.'

'I already did,' Lisa said with a tight little smile. She had hung up on him without answering, but it wouldn't do her any good, of course.

She could imagine without any difficulty whatever just what look the blue eyes had worn as he heard her slam the phone down. The more she struggled the more he would enjoy it. He always did.

CHAPTER TWO

EVAN lounged on the edge of Lisa's desk a week later skimming over a letter with a compressed mouth and irritated eyes. 'Hell, if he wasn't Anna's brother I'd kick him down the front steps with the greatest pleasure in the world!'

'He does try.' It was a pathetic response, but the only one she could give him, and his yellow eyes told her as much.

'You'd do a better job.' Evan's features softened into a mischievous grin. 'I guess you'd sell advertising without using a word of copy. One look at that figure and our clients would be queueing up to have you handle their accounts.' He winked. 'So long as they got to handle yours.'

Her icy face merely made him burst out laughing. He got up and threw down the letter. 'Tell Jon to keep out of my way today or I might just bang his head on a wall.'

When he had gone Lisa filed the letter of acid complaint from Renton and looked at Jon's closed door with compassion. He was having a bad week. Not quite as bad as hers, perhaps, but bad enough.

Her week had been flat and quiet and all the more disconcerting for that because that devil was keeping her guessing, and her mind was working overtime as she tried to anticipate his next move.

She had even begun to ask herself if he wasn't following up at all, and that was a dangerous sign because she knew it was wish-fulfilment of the weakest sort. If she let herself slacken in relief the shock would be all the more unbalancing when it came.

She was typing letters an hour later when Anna Wright walked into the room. Lisa smiled at her with pleasure. Anna had a calm, confident face with her brother's pale blue eyes and the curly fair hair thickened into a bright frame for her face. She was pregnant again. It was her third child, but it had not lessened her maternal solicitude for her brother. Anna was a caring woman. She worried about those she felt responsible for and she would go to endless length to be sure they were happy.

'How are things?' she asked now, and Lisa read the question behind the quiet words.

'Not too good.'

'Oh,' Anna sighed. 'Evan on the warpath again?'

'I heard some tribal whooping this morning,' Lisa admitted. 'But he didn't actually try to scalp him. He was being very circumspect—just hinted that if he set eyes on Jon today he might kick him out of the building, so I was to keep Jon away from him.'

Anna's warm mouth compressed. 'I see.'

Lisa watched her angry face. 'Don't blame Evan,' she said impulsively in warning. 'He's right, you know. Jon isn't cut out for advertising.'

'He'll learn,' Anna said stubbornly, easing her back with a hand at it, rubbing her spine slowly in the characteristic gesture of pregnancy.

'Evan's too demanding,' she said in a voice which boded ill for her husband. 'He will bellow at Jon, and it always terrifies him.'

Evan was the bellowing sort, Lisa pondered; a large heavy man with a bull-like neck and strong face, those fierce yellow eyes always leaping with energy and that voice roaring commands at a tremendous pace. Anna must have known what sort of man she was marrying and she couldn't complain if Evan's driving passion swept her brother out of his path. Evan relished his work. He had a brain which fuelled new ideas constantly. He leaped lightly from concept to another, fresh, alive, intuitive. Jon's plodding got on his nerves.

Anna looked pleadingly at her. 'Try to keep Evan out of his hair.'

It was the other way around, surely, Lisa thought, but she smiled and nodded. 'I'll try.'

Anna lingered, still rubbing her back, her body swollen with the coming baby but still attractive in her pretty pink smock. 'Jon wants to marry you, doesn't he? He told me so. Do you think he will?'

She did not press that too eagerly because Anna, for all her love for her brother, knew he was no ball of fire and one look at Lisa's curved sensuous body told her that Lisa would have had better offers.

Shrugging, Lisa said, 'I'm not in love with him, Anna. I like him, that's all.'

Anna looked curiously at her, searching her smooth-skinned face, then turned away with a faint sigh. Lisa was the sort of woman who could have wrenched Jon into shape if she had tried and Anna knew it

'Jon's perfect husband material,' she suggested hopefully. 'All he needs is the right woman.'

'That isn't me,' Lisa told her firmly.

'But you do like him.' Anna was capable of turning the slightest thing to her advantage. She had all the determination, tenacity, which Jon lacked. Sometimes Lisa wondered if Anna had got Jon's share of those qualities by some fluke of genetics. She gave Lisa a smile now, her eyes bright. 'Or you wouldn't go out with him.'

Lisa smiled back because she was unavoidably touched by the other woman's persistence and love for her brother. Anna went off and Lisa got on with her work until twelve. Lunch was a moveable feast in the agency. One slipped out when one could. Quite often Jon took Lisa to have lunch with a client he wanted to impress. She rarely failed to do that. Today she snatched a sandwich before going off to Oxford Street to buy some shoes. She took as long as necessary without worrying. Evan did not mind about actual working hours so long as the job got done to his satisfaction. It was past two when she got back to the office. She had arrived early and would be staying late.

She walked into the office, halting as she saw Evan there. Warily she stared at him, but he was smiling for once, and as she watched he slapped Jon on the back. 'I'll buy you a box of best Havanas for Christmas if you pull it off.'

Jon was flushed and looking incredulous, his eyes dazed. 'I'll do my best.'

A faint ironic flicker came into Evan's face, then he shrugged. 'You do that.' He did not sound too certain about it, though.

He turned to beam at Lisa, his leonine eyes gleaming. 'We've had a windfall. A fat new cat just strolled into our parlour and guess what he said he wanted? Jon himself to handle his account or it was all no deal!' Evan had an amazed, helpless amusement in his face. 'How's that for a surprise?'

She was delighted and turned to smile at Jon
eagerly. 'That's fantastic! Was it a client recommen-
dation?'

'I guess so,' Evan shrugged. 'I wasn't too clear
about that. I was so staggered I could only nod and
smile from ear to ear.'

The telephone rang in Jon's office and he loped
off to answer it. Evan gave Lisa a dry smile.

'He could really mess this one up, so try to feed
him ideas, will you? I want to be kept fully informed.
If Jon fails to come up with anything I'll have a go
and we can pass it off as his work.'

He was talking very softly, careful to keep his tone
too low for Jon to catch. He rubbed a hand over his
face, his eyes faintly tired.

'Thank God! It's come at the right time. I hate
to quarrel with Anna, especially when she's pregnant.' He gave her one of his wide, angry shrugs,
his sallow skin taut. 'She is as soft as butter where
that dumb-brained brother of hers is concerned. Until the baby arrives I want to keep her happy. If it
means I have to nurse Jon through every inch of this
deal, I'll do it if it kills me.'

'I'll do what I can,' she promised. She admired
Evan for his angry, impatient love for his wife. Evan
adored her, but sometimes felt like shaking her.
Everyone had a weak point, and Evan's was Anna.
However much she tried his patience, he would walk
through fire for her. Anna's weak point was Jon and
there was something extremely touching in the way
she worried over her helpless, vulnerable brother. It

was the same quality that made her an excellent mother to her two little boys.

It was something of a relief to Evan that his sons looked like him. 'I was scared stiff one of them might turn out to look like Jon,' he once confessed to Lisa. 'Anna and Jon look so alike. I had this sinking feeling that one of our kids might take after him, and I don't know how I would have put up with that.'

The boys, Andy and Tom, were dark and brown-eyed, with olive skins and clear, sharp voices. They already faced life with their father's dynamic energy. They fought like young dogs. Anna adored both of them. So did Evan, although he concealed it with offhand treatment, prone to bellow at them. The fact that they appeared to thrive on his rough handling deepened his pride in them. One of Jon's worst faults, Evan had once said to Lisa, was the way he flinched whenever Evan came into a room. 'It makes me want to kick him!' Evan had growled.

Now he studied the blue sky beyond the window with a smile. 'I wouldn't mind if Anna had a girl this time,' he said. 'One who looked like her.' His grimace was ironic. 'Jon should have been a girl, too, poor swine. He'd have made a great girl.'

Lisa bit back a smile. His heavy lids drooping, Evan studied her. 'What the hell do you see in him?'

He had asked her that before. He would probably ask her again. Lisa shrugged and smiled without replying.

'Women!' Evan threw his hands up to heaven in derisive comment. 'They're crazy!'

He slammed out of the office and a moment later

Magda sneaked into the room, her eyes alive with curiosity. 'What's all this about Jon getting a big account? Evan is bouncing around the office giving out cigars.'

'It's true. I don't know any details yet, though.'

'Evan will slit his throat and hang him up from a lamp post if he drops this one,' Magda informed her. 'So he says.'

'Evan says more than he means.' Lisa wasn't quite as confident as she sounded.

The afternoon sunlight slid stickily along the walls and fell in yellow pools on the pale carpet. She stared at it and wished she could make up her mind what to do. She had become involved with these people and that was a mistake. Get involved, and you're hooked. It isn't easy to walk away from people you've started to care about, especially when you already have an enormous problem in another direction. She could just take flight, of course, but running is a lonely business, and there was always the chance that he might pick up her trail again and repeat the whole process elsewhere. She couldn't keep running for ever.

'These stockings have a run, damn them!' Magda glumly extended her slim calf to inspect the place where the nylon had begun to run. 'I only put them on this morning!'

'I'll lend you a pair,' Lisa offered. 'Are you short of money already?'

'Aren't I always? You're a pet.' Magda grinned at her.

The door opened behind them and they both

glanced round. Lisa stood there and felt all her colour draining away, her body stiffening in terrified recognition.

Magda stayed, open-mouthed, in the same position while the amused, cynical blue eyes inspected her displayed leg. Then she hurriedly pulled down her skirt, flushing.

Evan had entered on Steve Crawford's heels. Seeing his client staring at Magda he automatically introduced her. Steve took Magda's hand, smiling down at her, the sleepy tigerish twist of his mouth making her blush deepen.

'Magda's from the art department,' Evan expanded.

One dark brow rising, Steve said: 'What a pity. I was hoping she would be working on our account.'

'No,' said Magda with a regret she didn't bother to disguise, and got another of his smiles, to which she responded with an electric glow.

Evan was looking more and more satisfied. He liked a client he could put into a labelled box, and he was putting Steve Crawford into one now. Reading Evan's smug smiles clearly, Lisa thought that Evan for once was having the wool pulled over his eyes. It was not an easy thing to do. Evan was sharp and knowledgeable about human nature. Steve Crawford just didn't happen to be the easily categorised male Evan was imagining him to be—you didn't put men like that into labelled boxes and then forget them. In some ways he could be predictable, it was true, but in other ways he was totally unreadable.

Waiting for the cool turn of that black head, Lisa

hoped she was looking as cool as he was, and doubted it. Her heart was going at a rate which made the hollow of her throat pulse visibly. He wouldn't miss that. He knew all the small signs of her physical reaction as well as she did.

When he finally turned, as though reluctant to look away from Magda, he let his glance drift over her face in apparent indifference. She stared coldly at him.

'Lisa Hartley, Jon's secretary,' said Evan with the triumphant air of a conjuror pulling a rabbit out of a hat. Lisa, in his experience, was guaranteed to have an effect on the most world-weary, disinterested male. Evan regarded her as a tremendous asset to the firm. That was why he kept her with Jon—as some sort of counterweight to Jon's ineptitude.

'Miss Hartley,' Steve said in that sleepy, leisured drawl which could so easily become the savage snap of a whiplash, and he emphasised her name with an intent none of those in the room could read, but which made her green eyes flare defiantly at him.

It was all a maddening charade, but she was trapped by her own desire not to drag that fact out into the open. She saw the spark of amusement in his eyes which revealed that he was revelling in her situation, and could have kicked him. She should have anticipated some such move as this on his part. The clever, devious swine had been looking around for some weapons before he came anywhere near her, and in Jon he had found one he thought might prove useful.

She watched Steve's face as he studied Jon's fair, nervous features. Evan tried to give a bright gloss to Jon's stricken dumbness in the face of the important client, but Steve's black brows hovered sardonically as Jon mumbled a few sentences at him.

'We'll need to have a few conferences with you,' Evan said in jovial emphasis. 'In fact, it would be useful if Jon could fly out and look around to get the feel of your image, test out the market.'

'Excellent,' Steve murmured, smiling.

Lisa's heart missed a beat. She caught the brief glance he threw in her direction.

'I'll make sure you get all the co-operation you need,' he went on softly. 'In fact, I'll be there myself to make certain of that.'

Evan slapped Jon on the back. 'California,' he said brightly. 'You lucky lad! I hope you won't forget you're there to work, not to enjoy yourself.' He laughed loudly to demonstrate that this was a joke, largely for Steve's listening ears. Jon did not look as though he was quite sure about that, though.

Crawford & Dent were a property firm in California who had a list of very exclusive clients and some high-priced properties in their control. Steve explained to Magda, who listened with fascination, that he wanted the firm's image buffed up.

Glancing at Evan, he added: 'I thought an outside view of us might come up with a new idea. It sometimes helps.'

Lisa's eyes lowered, angry rebellion in them. How could he stand there and lie like that? She heard Jon making soothing noises and Evan shifting his feet, almost visibly willing his brother-in-law to make an impression on his wealthy and desirable client. Jon was spinning out an optimistic web of promise to conceal his total lack of ideas, his voice nervous. *Poor Jon,* Lisa thought. *If he loses this account, Evan will skin him alive!*

'Yes, I see,' drawled Steve, considering him.

'Of course, there hasn't been time to come up with anything yet,' Evan rushed in hurriedly. 'Give us a few days, Mr Crawford.'

'Of course,' Steve encouraged, smiling at him. 'We must get to know each other before we get down to brass tacks.'

'Yes,' said Evan, relieved, laughing too loudly. 'We must certainly do that. I'd be delighted to have you to dinner at my home tonight, by the way. Jon will be there, won't you, Jon?' He patted his shoulder with the sideways look of one who would like to slap him flat. 'My brother-in-law, you know,' he told Steve. 'My wife's brother. We're a family concern, we work closely together. I help Jon out and he helps me.'

'How admirable,' Steve murmured with a tiny glint of the blue eyes, and then he turned to give Lisa the briefest glance. 'And Miss Hartley ... will she be dining with us?'

'Of course,' Evan said at once, remembering the box he had put Steve into at the beginning. He threw Lisa an encouraging smile which said openly: flatter him, please him, for God's sake keep him happy.

Steve intercepted that look, unfortunately, and

Lisa saw him interpreting it and suppressing a little smile.

Damn him, she thought, her green eyes flashing in rebellion, and Steve caught that look too, and smiled even more deeply, the lines at the side of his mouth giving him that characteristic look of sardonic amusement.

She could refuse to turn up, of course, but Evan would want to know why, and he would take her defection out on Jon. He would think that Jon hadn't persuaded her eloquently enough.

Steve knew. She caught his eyes watching her obliquely. He had somehow discovered all about Jon's precarious position here and her involvement with him, and Steve knew all about her inability to be ruthless with lame ducks. He would take all the advantage he could of her weakness.

If she had any sense she would run now, but Steve would be a step behind her. For all she knew he was having her watched. He had done before. What was the point in running? She would stand still and fight this time.

She would go to dinner and stick closely to Jon. It would be impossible for Steve to get at her with other people around. All he could do was dig at her and keep those mocking blue eyes fixed on her. That would be bad enough, of course, but she could take it.

Evan steered Steve towards the door, but Steve insisted on Evan and Jon going first. Then he waved Magda through the door, his smile making her flutter, while Lisa watched, hating him.

Before he went out he slid his eyes towards her. They wandered insolently from the wide, passionate mouth to the sway of her hips, and they didn't miss a thing.

He laughed silently at the glare she gave him and walked out. The game had hardly begun and already she was struggling like someone who has walked into a swamp and can't extricate themselves.

I hate him, she told herself thickly. I hate him!

Magda took a great interest in watching Lisa get ready for dinner that evening. She sat crouched on the bed, cross-legged, sighing enviously. 'Wasn't he just super? Those wicked eyes—I bet he gets his own way with eyes like that. I wish I was invited. Why didn't you suggest it to Evan?'

'Sorry.' Lisa smiled at her in the mirror and that smile cost her a good deal because she was very nervous. Her hands were shaking as she applied her make-up and she hoped Magda hadn't noticed because that would start speculation she did not want.

'Did you notice the way he sort of purrs when he talks? I never heard a sexier voice.'

Lisa's mouth tightened. 'I can't talk and put on make-up,' she snapped.

Magda barely heard her. 'I do wish I was going,' she said again.

I wish I wasn't, Lisa thought, eyeing her own reflection with guarded disapproval. It was a mistake to wear this dress. Steve liked her in black. She should have worn green or brown. He might think her choice of colour significant. Too late to change her mind now.

Jon was driving her to Evan's house. He would be here soon. She stood back and studied herself, mouth wry.

'Whew!' whistled Magda. 'You're wasted on Jon. Now if I were you, I'd go all out to catch Steve Crawford—he's not only rich, he's sexy, and he makes Jon look like a white rabbit.'

'I like white rabbits,' said Lisa with a wry appreciation of the irony of the lie.

'You know, that's the first time a good-looking man has ever looked at me first when you were around,' said Magda, her voice excited. 'Do you think he fancied me?'

Lisa smiled, hiding her faint sadness. 'Maybe he did. You were giving a pretty floor show at the time, I seem to remember.'

Magda giggled. 'Funny, wasn't it? He didn't seem shocked.'

Lisa's brows lifted. 'You've got to be joking. He loved it.'

She left Magda wearing a wide smile, but she herself was not amused. Steve had played that scene deliberately, pretending not to see her and keeping her waiting, knowing how he was tying her nerves into knots.

Jon looked at her with satisfaction. 'You look fabulous. Now, Evan asked me to remind you to be extra nice to Crawford.' His smile was teasing. 'Not too nice, of course, but that's my request, not Evan's.'

'Had any ideas yet?' she asked without much hope.

'A few.' Jon was guarded at once and the stiff lines into which his face fell worried her. He was hiding his total lack of ideas and that meant it was going to be hard to get him to admit the truth.

When they arrived at Evan's large mock-Tudor house they were met by Anna in a cream lace smock dress in which she somehow managed to look quite fetching despite her obviously pregnant appearance. Her hair had been done that afternoon, her face expertly made up. She threw Lisa a complimentary, relieved smile as she took in the sophistication of her dress and the sensuous gleaming gloss of her face and hair.

'Wonderful!' Having disposed of that she turned with reproving eyes to her brother. 'Had any ideas yet?'

Jon looked mulish. 'Some.'

He slid past her and Lisa gave Anna a wry smile. 'Is he telling the truth?' Anna demanded, and Lisa shrugged.

The frown which creased Anna's forehead made her look pale and gloomy. Lisa put an arm round her. 'Forget it. I'll see it comes out all right.'

'Will you?' Anna brightened. 'Evan is watching him like a tiger watching a piece of meat. Oh, why can't Jon buck himself up?' She rubbed one finger across her brow as though erasing that row of small lines. 'I do so want him to get on! I'm sure he could do it if he tried.'

Jon was a square peg in a round hole, but Anna was never going to admit that and Jon hadn't got the guts to tell her he was getting out and go. He would

go on weakly struggling and Evan would fume while
Anna wept and begged and shouted at him to be
kind to her baby brother.

What Jon needed, Lisa thought, was to meet a
woman stronger than Anna who would march up to
her and tell her frankly to let go of Jon or she would
bat her on the head with something. Anna would,
Lisa sensed, be quite relieved if and when that happened. Until then, she would continue doing good
to Jon whether it made him happy or not.

It was almost as if Anna was trying to jog Jon into
taking on Evan when it was obvious to anyone with
half an eye that Evan could eat him for breakfast
and never notice. Anna loved Evan. She loved Jon,
too. But she had set them at each other's throats right
from the first and she did not seem aware of what
she was doing. If she once let Jon go and he got out
of Evan's own back yard, the brothers-in-law might
actually get on quite well, but Anna persisted in trying to whip Jon into meeting Evan on his own
ground when it was all a dead loss from the start.

Or was Jon a cross which she was laying on Evan's
broad shoulders in an attempt to get him to prove
his love for her? Certainly, Evan's irritated patience
with Jon over the years demonstrated clearly the
measure of his love for his wife. Evan would so
dearly have loved to boot Jon out of the firm long
ago.

With her arm through Lisa's, Anna led her into
the sitting-room and the men all rose. Lisa had
suited her walk to the slow roll of Anna's rotund
body, but as she advanced into the room she felt

those mocking eyes on the supple, sensuous sway of her body. They took their time in making a detailed inventory like someone checking stock to make sure none of it was missing.

Across the room she forced herself to meet his eyes. His lids were half-down, his bones sharp under that gleaming brown skin, his lips straight but with something in the tension of them which made her whole body shake.

Evan's sister, Catherine, was the third woman, and she had to have been invited for Jon because with her heavy features and leonine eyes which were so like her brother's, she was certainly not the sort of bait Evan would provide for a client he suspected liked women. Catherine had been brought along to make up the numbers and her sulky face said she knew it.

Jon guessed that, too. He was standing beside her now, his mouth turned down at the edges, but he wasn't making any move to change matters. He was accepting Evan's decree.

To make quite sure that everyone knew the position, Evan took her hand now and led her across to Steve. 'You remember, Steve, you met Lisa this afternoon at the office.'

Steve's amused eyes held a gleam. 'I remember, of course,' he said. 'Hallo, Lisa.'

'Hallo,' she said with a burning desire to pick up the whisky bottle from the table and slam it over his head.

CHAPTER THREE

CONVERSATION was light and easily kept rolling. Evan saw to that. He had a quick, clever mind and he was never slow to come back with a remark which made Steve's eyes glint with amusement. The two men got on, and if Jon's occasional lame remark was ignored, it was all done with civility, and Anna did not need to bristle with offended annoyance.

She was talking mainly to Catherine, who was a devoted aunt, perhaps because at thirty-seven she had begun to doubt if she would marry herself and was turning her attention to her nephews. Catherine had a sullen temperament. She lacked her brother's quickness and wit. The pale dress she wore did nothing for her rather heavy looks and she wore the wrong make-up for her sallow skin.

She did not like Lisa and saw no reason for hiding it. Lisa ignored the friction which Catherine encouraged between them and got grateful smiles from Anna every now and then in consequence. Catherine could be very difficult.

It was over dinner that Lisa realised with a sinking heart that Jon was drinking too much. She glanced at Anna to point this out to her, but Anna was deep in talk with Steve, who was bending those wicked eyes on her face and bringing a sparkle to Anna's blue eyes. Although she adored Evan she wasn't immune to a smile like that one, thought Lisa. Who was?

Drink always conferred a temporary confidence on Jon, which might be why he sometimes drank too much, an idea which struck cold in Lisa's mind, wondering if this tendency would grow as he got older and came more and more to depend upon the crutch of alcohol to get him through the day.

Now he was talking quite brightly, smiling with blue eyes that had a glazed brilliance, and Anna appeared blind to it, looking at him with fond assurance, pleased by his sudden display of certainty.

He outlined an idea which had some possibilities and Steve's long fingers drummed on the edge of the table as he nodded and listened.

'Not bad,' he said, while Evan watched him eagerly.

'We could work on that,' Evan suggested.

'Toss a few more ideas into the hat first,' said Steve blandly. He flicked a look at Jon as he lifted his glass to his mouth. Lisa saw the slow rise of Steve's brows and cursed him. Evan and Anna might not have noticed Jon's drinking, but Steve had, and the curl of his mouth told her he was amused by it.

He had always had a sharp grasp of character and he used it ruthlessly. Leaning forward, he picked up his own glass and sipped. Jon followed suit yet again and his glass emptied. Steve smiled at him. 'Yes, I quite like that idea of yours,' he said, and casually filled Jon's glass again.

Lisa glared at him. The mocking eyes flicked to her and Steve smiled. Under the tablecloth her hands curled in her lap. She would like to rake her nails down his grinning face. How could he be such a swine?

'How long are you over here?' asked Evan.

'That depends.' Steve did not look at Lisa, but she felt his attention deeply. 'I have a little business to complete. When that's dealt with I'll go back to the States.'

Evan tilted his glass before he drank. 'Good luck with it, then.'

Jon did the same. 'Good luck,' he said thickly.

Steve smiled and turned his eyes to Lisa. 'Aren't you going to drink to the success of my business?' he asked her with a faint taunt in his voice.

The others picked it up and looked at them in surprise. Lisa gave him a tight little smile, her wide passionate mouth parted over white teeth. 'I'm sure you don't need luck,' she told him with her hand resolutely not gripping her glass.

'Maybe not,' he agreed very smoothly. 'I always get what I want in the end.'

Not this time, she thought, and her defiant eyes told him what she was thinking, then she did pick up her glass and drink, her head back, the full bright cloud of her hair rustling against her shoulders, her long throat lifted as she tilted the glass in a sinuous movement which kept Steve's eyes fixed on her and made them harden into a fierce darkness which ate her across the table.

The others were talking, laughing, not noticing. Lowering her glass, Lisa met his eyes with defiance, forcing down the rapid pulsing in her body which his stare precipitated.

After dinner she sat beside Jon, who was very flushed and could only mumble the occasional word. His hand groped round her waist and pulled her close to him. She deliberately leaned there, his fingers under the high warm swell of her breasts, and let herself outstare Steve who was retaining his smile but had a narrow glint in his eye as he watched Jon touch her.

Lisa turned her head to smile at Jon and her hair brushed softly across his cheek, the fragrance of it filling his nostrils. He put up a shaky hand to touch the satin curve of her cheek. She had rarely seen any excitement in him, but there was the flicker of it in his eyes now and she sensed that it was bred by her own inner excitement. He had unwittingly picked up the powerful sexual turmoil within her and was unconsciously affected by it.

Her black lashes swept down over her over-bright green eyes. She felt Jon lean over and touch her lips lightly before moving away.

Evan looked irritated. He had intended to keep Crawford happy by dangling Lisa in front of him, but for once Jon was deliberately defying him, and with Anna watching, Evan didn't dare do anything.

The talk and laughter was growing flatter. Catherine kept looking at her watch. Evan had been throwing ideas at Steve in the hope of seeing him snap at one, but Steve had been blandly noncommittal.

Then Steve rose and glanced at his watch. 'It's been a very pleasant evening, Mrs Wright. I've enjoyed it enormously, but now I'm afraid I should be off. Can I give anybody a lift?' He glanced at Catherine, who said in her stiff way that she was staying the night with her brother.

Steve turned his glance on Lisa, who said brightly, 'Jon will drive me home, thank you.'

'Will he?' The arch of the saturnine brows was sufficient. Lisa turned dismayed eyes on Jon and found him fast asleep, his mouth partly open.

'Oh, no!' she exclaimed, and cut the panic off before Steve heard it. 'I can get a taxi,' she said hurriedly.

'Nonsense.' Steve was amused, a leisurely hand detaching her from Jon and raising her to her feet. 'My car's outside.'

Anna looked at her brother with dismay and Evan with suppressed rage. Lisa found herself moving to the door with that long hand curled around her arm and no escape.

The night was cloudy. A crescent moon slid silently in and out like a needle being threaded through the sky, drawing a fine silver thread of moonlight after it. 'Goodnight,' Anna called as they walked away. The soft light from the house was giving the darkness definition as the wind rustled through the trees on either side of them.

Lisa's throat was tight and hot. She pulled her arm out of Steve's grip as soon as they were out of sight of the house and stopped dead, turning angry eyes on him.

'I'm not going home with you!'

'Aren't you, honey?' When he used that term his voice took on the deep sensual purr which Magda had described and which always made Lisa's blood run faster.

'No, Steve,' she said, her eyes spitting at him, green as grass between their black lashes.

'No?' Although it was a question the word was really an answer, teasing, confident.

'Swine!' she muttered, her head bent. A prolonged struggle in this quiet suburban street was not her idea of fun.

'Such a limited vocabulary, my darling,' Steve taunted with a gleam in those blue eyes and a husky deep softness in his voice which made her temperature rise.

'I hate the sight of you!' Sometimes she almost convinced herself she did. The cynical eyes, the sensual mouth, could repel as well as attract her, reminding her of things she preferred to forget.

His car was a graceful object, as sleek as its owner, gleaming silver in the moonlight, looking for all the world like a crouched white cat. It purred like Steve too with a deep repressed growl of energy as he started the ignition. He would have hired it for his stay in England. The cars he drove in California were elongated, gleaming things with engines that raced and ate up the miles at a fantastic speed. He liked speed.

'You know where I live,' Lisa said pointedly.

His sideways grin was silent.

Infuriated, she spat suddenly, 'Can't you take no for an answer?'

'I might—if you meant it.'

'I do!' She spoke with vehemence, but his unconcerned smile told her he refused to believe her. Shaking with temper, she looked away and suddenly realised that they were not heading in the direction of her flat. They were on the Embankment, the Victorian globes of the lamps shedding their diffused pale light on the pavement. 'This isn't the way.' She turned to look at him and he was whistling through his teeth, the long hands spinning the wheel without effort.

'Take me home, Steve.'

He turned his black head and smiled at her. Her heart missed a beat.

'Steve!' She muttered it angrily.

'My darling?'

'Don't call me that! Take me home.'

'Why haven't you told Lister about us?'

The question stopped her. She shrank back in her seat. 'You're kidding!'

'None of them at the agency know a thing about you, do they?'

'You think I'd broadcast it to the world?' The bitterness was seeping into her voice although she tried to keep it calm.

He glanced into his driving mirror as another car blazed past, headlights full on, dazzling them. 'Silly devil.' He looked back at her. 'I wonder what reaction you'll get when Lister does find out about us.'

'I suppose you're going to tell him?'

Steve used any weapon he had to and she had realised at once that her own silence at the agency had put one weapon in his hands. She was not looking at him now, staring into the empty night with bitter eyes, but she felt his long, considering stare. He had a delicate awareness of the amount of pressure it was safe to bring. He handled people like an expert dismantling bombs.

'Ah well,' he said after a moment, 'I suppose Wright won't mind losing that contract too much.'

She stiffened. 'You blackmailing swine!'

He smiled. 'Me?'

'You're threatening to take away the contract, aren't you?'

'Oh, no,' he protested silkily. 'But do you think Lister will want to work for me once he knows I was ...' He paused, as though searching for the right word, his face wickedly amused. 'What did you once call me? Your owner?'

Her cheeks flamed and her hands curled into fists, moving restlessly on her lap.

'I'm only using your own words,' he said, pretending bafflement at her rage, innocence in the slide of his eyes.

'I'd like to cut your throat!'

He laughed softly. 'I believe you.' The blue eyes had a narrow, intimate smile in them as they watched her. 'You've always had a red-hot temper to go with that hair.'

The quarrel had occupied the forefront of her mind and she hadn't noticed that they were now driving into a deep underground car park until the yellow overhead lights forced themselves upon her attention.

Sitting upright, she said furiously, 'Take me home, Steve.'

'I am, honey,' he murmured with that glinting little smile.

As he parked the car with ease she turned on him, her hand slapping his face. He caught her wrists, held them down at her side, bent her back so that his lowered head was directly over her own. The blue eyes warned coolly.

'You know better than that, my darling. Don't you ever learn? I don't take slaps from anybody.'

'I'm not going in there!' He was hurting her, the arch of her back painful, but it was fear of something else which was making her ache from head to foot.

He didn't answer, but his slow smile spoke for him. Lisa writhed in his hands and hated the way he watched her supple, twisting body.

His head lowered very slowly and his lips silkily touched her throat for a second. 'Honey, I'm starving for you.'

She closed her eyes. Not this time, she told herself again. Oh, God, give me the strength to say no to him. She couldn't let him take her in there because however hard she tried to resist him once he started touching her she would be lost, helpless, unable to refuse him anything he wanted.

'I'm not coming in,' she repeated, as though it were some sort of magic phrase, a talisman which might ward him off.

'Well,' Steve murmured lazily, 'I could carry you, but that would cause a little talk. I guess we'll have to manage down here.'

Her eyes flew open and she looked at him in raging incoherence. 'Don't touch me!'

'It's been a long time, honey,' he said with the faintest unsteadiness as he bent his head.

The pattern was always the same, a fight between them which had always ended the same way. Steve would not stop until he had made her yield, admit her own inability to resist him. She kept her lips closed tightly under the demanding lips, thrust at his covering body with her hands, twisting and writhing in his arms and only deepening his excitement and arousing her own.

Angrily she felt the rising heat inside herself and redoubled her efforts to escape before she lost control. There had to be a way of fighting how he made her feel. If only she could find it.

He was coaxing her lips to open for him, his mouth seductive, while the long fingers played over her body, teasing and tormenting her, knowing their way so intimately, knowing exactly how to please and arouse her.

'Darling,' he whispered into her ear, his lips caressing, his breath warm as he explored the sensitive crevices before he slid his mouth down her neck and then returned to her mouth.

She felt as though she were on the point of tears. Tired, drained, her eyes closed heavily and at once her control over herself lapsed. Her lips parted, her body yielded itself to his hands.

He gave a muffled groan, hungrily exploring the
mouth under his own, and his hand twined itself
into the thick cloud of her hair, finding her nape
and pulling her closer to him, while his other hand
ran down the curve of her body in a possessive movement.

Her hands slid up his chest and went round his
neck. She moaned, kissing him back, twisting against
him, aware of the flame beating higher in her body.

Steve lifted his head and his half-closed eyes
flashed over her. 'That's better. Now we'll go in, shall
we?'

She snapped out of it, shuddering. 'No!'

His mouth hardened. 'Don't make me lose my
patience.'

She pushed him away and sat up, running a trembling hand through her hair. 'I told you no and I
meant it.'

'You never mean it,' he said, his eyes flicking
contemptuously over her. 'It didn't take me long,
did it, Lisa?' He lifted his arm and glanced deliberately at his watch. 'Ten minutes, that's all it
took.'

That went home like a knife. 'Take me home or
I'll walk.' The green eyes were molten with bitter
feeling.

He smiled unpleasantly. 'Oh, not yet. We've got
some talking to do. We can do it here if you insist
or we can do it in more comfort in my flat.'

'You think I'm stupid enough to let you lure me
in there?' She looked at him angrily. 'And we've
got nothing to talk about.'

Steve was as furious as herself, but his voice was thick with the desire she could still read in those blue eyes. 'We're going to discuss terms, Lisa,' he said huskily.

'Your terms!' She knew what those terms would be and her teeth sank into her lower lip in an effort to stop her mouth shaking.

He smiled. 'Oh, yes, my terms. Of course. You can do this the easy way or you can do it the hard way, it's up to you. I'll get what I want in the end. I always do.'

Silently she shook her head. He smiled again, ice in his face. 'What did you think you would achieve by running back to England? You knew I wouldn't let it rest there. You've known all along that I wa behind you and that one day I'd catch up with you.'

Yes, she had known. She stared at him and the colour drained from her face. He was remorseless; unforgetting, unforgiving.

Looking away, she tried for the last time. It would be the last time, she told herself. She would never say this again.

'I was not going away with him, Steve. I didn't know what was in his mind. He said he was taking me to the apartment, but he kept on driving and he was going too fast. I begged him to take me back and he wouldn't listen.'

Steve merely looked bored. 'I seem to have heard this story before,' he drawled. 'It's no more convincing this time. Harrison was your lover for weeks before that crash. Bad luck for you that the police got in touch with me when they discovered who you were, wasn't it?'

'Bad luck for me I wasn't killed along with Denny,' she said in abrupt pain.

Steve's face hardened. He turned and started the engine, backing with a screech of tires which echoed in the great concrete cave. The yellow overhead lights flashed past at a terrific rate. They were out in the moonlit night before she had a chance to think.

Steve had a guard on his temper most of the time. He had always been coolly controlled, even when he was angry, and that had often maddened her, particularly at the period in their relationship when he had treated her with carefully conscious cruelty.

His temper had slipped now, though. As he drove she saw the furious flash of the blue eyes, the hard compression of his mouth. The mockery and menacing amusement had gone, leaving his face a taut mask filled with rage.

He had regained his temper by the time they reached her flat. He switched off the engine and turned to her with a grim coolness. 'You're lucky my self-control is so good. Don't ever say anything of the sort to me again. You belong to me. You're a treacherous, unfaithful little bitch, but you aren't ever going to look at another man again. I'm taking you back where you belong, and when I've got you there I'm going to lock you up and throw away the key.'

Her voice shook. 'If you believe I'm all those things, why do you want me?'

'Because you're mine,' he said through his teeth.

'Human beings don't belong to anyone,' she snapped furiously.

'You belong to me.'

Lisa's spine prickled with rage at the assertion. She eyed him with positive hatred, seeing the strongly moulded lines of his face with repulsion. He had always been a possessive, tenacious man with a fierce will towards enforcing his own personality on the people with whom he came into contact. He had been born into a wealthy Californian family, educated to take up a position of power. The desire for power was bred in his bones, he had taken it in with his mother's milk.

'Nothing I own ever gets away from me,' he said with those hard blue eyes locked on to her flushed and angry face.

The way he had been brought up had taught him to cloak his thirst for power with a silken manner which charmed opponents into imagining that he could be coaxed and persuaded. Steve smiled a good deal, his blue eyes seductive when he chose. Lisa had often seen women fluttering like hypnotised birds with those blue eyes smiling at them, and it had always infuriated her. The smooth charm was so totally artificial and yet so damned convincing. She thought of the way he had smiled at Magda in the office, making the other girl quiver with excitement and a mistaken belief that Steve fancied her. Steve used people ruthlessly as weapons when he found it necessary.

It had not taken her long to realise that the glossy

façade he presented to the world covered a nature
of iron intention. Steve had a very clear idea of
what he wanted and where he was going and he
merely covered his ruthlessness with silky charm because he had learnt that people were far more ready
to accept power when it was disguised from them.

She glared back at him, her face stiff with rebellion.
'I belong to myself!'

His eyes ran down over her in an all-too-familiar
fashion. 'You told me so yourself once; you said I
was your owner, and that's what I am, Lisa. I
bought you, and what I buy stays bought, even if it
proves to be worthless.'

She winced at that and he caught the little movement, his mouth sardonic. 'Yes,' he said, 'worthless.
A cheap, easy little bitch ...'

She hit him and he wrenched her hand down,
twisting her arm behind her back, watching her
with leaping eyes. 'I won't tell you again. Don't hit
me.'

'I won't ever come back with you,' she whispered
shakily. 'You're wasting your time.'

Steve's mouth twisted into a mimicry of a smile.
'Oh, yes, you will, my darling. Sooner or later you're
going to give in because you've never been able to
say no to a man in your life.'

The irony of that ate into her. She had said no to
Denny and to every man she met before she met
Steve, but Steve just would not believe that after the
car crash. Denny had been so good to her for years.
He had built up her career selflessly and when she
realised that he was in love with her she had been

able to feel nothing but pity. Pity was the most destructive of the emotions, the most dangerous. She should never have weakened towards Denny. She should have ruthlessly kept him at a distance, shut him out of her life as though he were an enemy.

She had not been able to—her old fondness for him, her compassion for the violence of his feeling for her, had left her behaviour wide open to misinterpretation.

Denny had believed she cared for him. While Steve was away on that last trip, Denny had driven her away on a pretence of taking her home and when she realised they were not heading in the right direction she had not realised exactly what he meant to do for some time. Then she had pleaded, when she should have become angry. She had been deeply sorry for him when she should have told him sharply to take her home.

'You love me,' Denny had cried, his eyes fierce, and she had been speechless.

The crash had happened a few moments later. Lisa had been strapped into the car, but Denny, in his excitement, hadn't worn his safety belt. She was bruised and cut and had a broken arm, but Denny had been thrown through the windscreen and killed instantly.

Steve had looked at her with the eyes of a savage stranger. Her denials had been greeted with contempt. 'Don't lie to me. He was your lover. How often did you have these cosy weekends when I was away? I used to ring you in the evening and get no answer, but I was too stupid to work that one out.

Blind of me, wasn't it? And so convenient for you and Harrison.'

'No, Steve,' she had groaned, 'it isn't true. Denny was never my lover.'

She had blithely thought at first that she would be able to convince him in time. When her injuries healed and she was fit Steve took her to the cottage in Florida. It was only gradually that the full misery of her situation dawned on her. Steve used her with a mixture of bitter contempt and desire. She hoped for a while that her passionate response would convince him she loved him, had never been unfaithful.

Steve had had detectives investigating Denny. He had discovered that he had rented a cottage in the hills, that they had been headed for it when they crashed. Lisa had been away and her case was in the car. So was a suitcase of Denny's things. All the evidence had pointed to infidelity. Steve's detectives had also come up with evidence from Denny's neighbours to the effect that Lisa was always at his apartment. She couldn't deny that. After all, she and Denny had worked together for years; it was just another assignment they had been going to on this last occasion.

Steve hadn't suggested divorce. On the contrary, he had told her he would put every obstacle in her way if she tried to get a divorce. He meant to keep her, but the way he treated her made her wish she was dead. She went through a whole range of reactions, from weeping to anger, from passionate response to a furious refusal to let him touch her, none of it affected him. He forced her again and again to submit to him and gradually she began to shake whenever she saw him. Her inability to resist made those blue eyes glitter with cynical contempt. He made love to her as though she were a woman he had picked up in the street, and in time that was how she felt. She almost began to believe in her own guilt. That was when she decided to run. Using her old passport, she had got back to England under her maiden name and found this job.

It had been a quiet refuge, but now it could no longer shelter her. Steve watched her white, shaken face and laughed softly. 'You look as if you need a drink, my darling.'

Lisa got out of the car and tore down to her front door. Steve did not follow. She heard him drive away and let herself into the flat. In the kitchen she made herself some strong black coffee. She needed to think.

The phone rang as she was leaning on the couch drinking the coffee. She snatched it up at the first ring.

'I thought it might make it easier for you to get to sleep if I assured you I wasn't going to tell Lister about us.' He hadn't identified himself, but that deep voice couldn't be anyone else.

'Thanks,' Lisa said tartly.

'Will you?'

She looked at the receiver and wished it was his throat. She'd squeeze until he stopped breathing.

'Goodnight,' she said, and slammed it down.

He knew she wouldn't tell Jon unless she had to —he had been teasing her again.

The last thing she wanted to do was to try to explain to Jon the complicated tangle of her life. It wasn't exactly her favourite subject. Of course, it could be made to sound quite simple, deadly simple. No doubt that was how Steve would tell it. Or would he?

She finished her coffee and sat there staring at nothing in particular, asking herself questions to which she did not know the answers, and getting answers to which she did not know the questions. There was an ache in the pit of her stomach and her only balm was her certain knowledge that Steve was suffering from the same problem. Aroused desire was a tortuous thing. It twisted inside her now like a trapped animal, clawing her.

If he came back. She stopped that sentence with a grim smile. When he came back—that was more like it. Was she going to be able to go on saying no when every instinct in her body screamed yes?

In the past, her body always won, at the expense of her mind, and Steve had ruthlessly used that treacherous accomplice to fulfil his own desire. She had grown very sick of self-contempt and humiliation. No matter how many times she told herself it would never happen again, it always did. When it came to it, she was helpless to force down the stupid, aching hunger of her physical need for him. She had walked out on him and meant it to be for ever, and then as soon as he had her in his arms she was melting, yielding, making sheer moonshine of all her brave statements about ending it.

This time, she told herself, this time I'm not going to be so weak.

Jon had red-rimmed eyes and a hangover next morning. Lisa didn't ask him how he felt—that was obvious. When she closed one of the drawers too sharply, she caught his wince and the hand going up to his head as though he were afraid it might fall off. Jon had a nasty headache. But of course, there was more to it than that. She didn't need to have it spelt out. When Evan passed her in the corridor he had a hunched impatience in his shoulders and his face was surly. He was furious with Jon again. Jon had got drunk and put at risk a valuable contract.

Feeling sorry for him, Lisa dropped some soluble aspirin into a glass of water and handed it to Jon. He drank the stuff, sighing. 'I'm in the doghouse,' he said heavily.

She didn't really want to know. She didn't want to get even more involved with them all. People were like spiders who spun fine glistening strands around one, if one let them, forcing one into a relationship which meant one was concerned, pushed into trying to help them. Although Jon was weaker than most he was a more industrious spider—his vulnerability spun durable strands. She looked at him ruefully.

She had to ask, after all. 'What happened?'

He lifted his tired shoulders and let them slump. 'Evan practically got me by the throat and throttled me this morning. Anna cried. Then she shouted. Evan shouted.' He ran his hands into his hair. 'I just sat there. What could I say? I was under pressure last night. I was so bloody desperate to make an impression on Crawford and then I blew it by getting drunk.'

'He didn't seem bothered.' Lisa couldn't tell him the truth. Of course Steve hadn't been bothered. He'd deliberately pushed Jon into getting drunk. It had given Steve the chance to get her alone and that was what he had been angling for—Steve knew she was trying to avoid him and he knew he had to use a more circuitous route than he had in the past. She had been very specific last time. 'Never again or I'll kill you,' she had said. 'Or myself.'

None of that was anything to do with Jon. He was just caught in the undertow, but she hated to see the drawn lines of his face as sunlight illuminated them for her.

Jon said wryly, 'I don't suppose he'd tell you what he thought, anyway.'

Steve didn't need to tell her. She knew. She knew more about the clever, tortuous processes of that brain than anyone in the world, probably, apart from Steve himself. She had known him for three years, after all; years during which they had fought, hated, made violent love and been deadly enemies. A human being had more sides than the naked eye can absorb, and Lisa knew a good many of Steve's.

'He seemed to me to be quite interested in one or two of the ideas you gave him last night.' That was true, anyway. Jon had come up with some semblance of a portfolio last night—under the sharpening influence of drink, admittedly, but he had done it. Evan must have forgotten that.

'I can't remember a damned thing.' Jon looked horrified, clasping his fair head.

'I remember,' she said, and he looked up at her with gratitude and relief.

'You do? My God, you angel! Can you let me have them typed out to show to Evan this morning?'

'I'll do it now.' She smiled and got a real smile back. Jon took her hand and kissed it.

'Thank you, Lisa.'

She practised a little sleight of hand on him as she typed out the ideas—improving on Jon's original conceptions wherever she could think of something to tighten them up. When she had finished she read it through, feeling satisfied. It would put Evan back into a good temper, anyway. He would remember these suggestions from last night, so he would think Jon had remembered them too. She reminded Jon to let Evan think he had and Jon nodded soberly.

One of her brighter additions was a list of suggested slogans. Jon laughed as he read them but made a face afterwards. 'Evan will never believe I produced these.'

'Maybe he won't notice,' she said. 'Several of them were yours, I'm sure. One or two were thrown out by Evan—that will put him in a good mood if he remembers.'

Jon went along to Evan's office with the papers and came back half an hour later looking far more cheerful.

'How did it go?' she asked.

'Fantastic.' Jon was flushed and bright-eyed now. 'Evan liked the ideas and he's sending them to Craw-

ford this morning. Crawford apparently took no
offence last night. He never mentioned my getting
drunk when he talked to Evan an hour ago. But he
did give out invitations to a party he's giving in the
flat he's rented, so the deal is still open.'

I bet it is, Lisa thought savagely. A party. How
predictable of Steve! He wasn't giving up and he
wasn't going away. Sometimes she thought he never
would and she would be trapped in this bitter web
for the rest of her life.

If Steve directly invited her out she would refuse.
So he was playing it in this devious fashion, knowing
the set-up here, which undoubtedly meant he had
hired someone to probe into her life in London. He
knew her too damned well. She was old enough, for
heaven's sake, to learn not to get so involved with
people. It was always a mistake. Sometimes it was
downright dangerous. That had been the cause of the
hellish period in her life which culminated in that
week in Florida.

She had once loved Florida, spending weeks there,
lying on the sand and soaking up sun while she
watched the surfers rolling on those great white-
crested waves, brown bodies appearing and disap-
pearing in graceful swoops like swallows, until they
lost that godlike grace and came to earth as the sea
shed them.

Now the very mention of the name could make her
feel sick. Steve had destroyed it for her. He had almost destroyed her. All human beings were a collection of scraps of self-respect, fear, doubt, pride and
all the other imaginable elements of human nature.

He had stripped Lisa of every feeling but self-disgust and he had created a vacuum into which she could only push a hatred for him which served to stiffen her back into some semblance of a human being.

She would not want anyone to know the depths into which she had fallen. It had been bad enough to touch the bottom without anybody knowing about it. Except Steve. He knew, of course. She hadn't been able to hide it from him and he had watched her falling every inch of the way with a ruthless intensity, as though the sight of her despair gave him a tortured pleasure.

Looking at Jon, she thought that it was far too easy to destroy someone. All one had to do was take away their self-respect and one was knocking away the pin which held them together. People were rarely conscious of doing it. Anna was blithely unaware that she was undermining her beloved brother. She would be deeply offended if Lisa hinted at it. Anna was a strong, active woman with a powerful drive. She had long ago begun the process of driving Jon, doing his thinking for him, creating his opportunities and groaning when he lost them.

Anna loved Jon. That was what made it all so painful. Anna was not self-aware. She did not probe her own motives or examine the results of what she did with such high intentions. When Steve set out to smash Lisa into little bits he did it consciously. He knew what he was doing and he meant it to happen under his eyes. It had made of that sunlocked seascape a dark prison, a torture chamber, from which Lisa had reeled in broken despair. His mock-

ing amusement had been the final touch. At least if
Anna ever did glimpse what she was doing to Jon she
would be horrified, self-reproachful. She wouldn't
laugh.

CHAPTER FOUR

Oɴ the Saturday morning Lisa was doing the housework, in a pair of jeans, an old shirt and a heavy-
backed plastic apron, when she heard a ring at the door
bell. Magda had taken a large bag of washing down to
the launderette a few streets away. They had worked
out their Saturday morning routine from the first week
in the flat. Lisa enjoyed doing housework, Magda did
not, so it was common sense for them to split up their
necessary tasks in this way.

Imagining that this was the milkman calling for his
money, she picked up her purse and went to the door.
She would have closed it at once when she saw who
was outside, but his foot wedged it open and his smile
mocked her.

'Go away!' she said sharply.

'I'm taking you to lunch,' Steve answered as if her
hostile tone had never reached him.

'No!'

He moved suddenly. Without her knowing quite
how it happened, the door was flying wide open and
he was inside the flat, lifting her out of his path as
though she were a doll, his hands firm on her slim
waist.

He put her down and closed the door, and she fell back, her heart thudding. They were alone and she felt suddenly cold. Her whole body began to tremble, and Steve did not miss it, his quick oblique glance and the flicker of his lashes as he looked away again, telling her that he had noted the reaction she could neither suppress nor disguise. His face tautened and although he had quite deliberately set out to hurt and humiliate her during that hellish period in Florida, she saw the compression of his mouth and knew it annoyed him to see her flinch away from him.

He pushed his hands into his pockets and strolled coolly around the room, throwing a curious eye over her books and the rack of records beside the record player. The flat was furnished in appalling taste—their landlord had, Lisa and Magda suspected, bought all the furniture at a jumble sale. Steve's brows lifted in ironic comment as he inspected it.

'How on earth do you live like this?'

It was a derisive question. Their home had been both elegant and luxurious; a very spacious and beautifully appointed apartment with every modern convenience including some electronic gadgets she had never used and did not miss.

'There are worse things than shabby furniture,' she told him with cold emphasis, her green eyes steady on his face.

He swung to survey her, his brows drawn. 'You've changed your mind, have you?'

The question bewildered her. Eyes wide open, she gazed back at him, frowning.

'That was why you married me in the first place,

wasn't it? For the money? You were a very ambitious girl. You played your cards cleverly, holding
me off until I was desperate enough to marry you.
Was it Harrison's idea? Did the two of you plan to
live on the alimony you would get when you finally
divorced me?'

On the point of bursting into an angry denial she
drew back and shrugged without answering.

'Are you admitting it?' His voice was level and
controlled, but the blue eyes were dangerous, molten
with anger and another emotion which she was not
quite certain she recognised.

'I admit nothing. Will you please go? I'm not going to lunch with you and I don't want you here.'

Steve stared at her without moving or speaking for
a long moment. She saw the gradual easing of his
taut features and knew he was dragging himself
back from the edge of a violent explosion. Turning
on his heel, he threw another look around the room.

'Does Lister come here?'

'Sometimes,' she said coolly.

The dark head swung back. 'He's another Harrison, isn't he? One of the lame ducks you collect so
avidly. What do you see in them? Does it give you
an egotistic thrill to know a man is weaker than
you are? Do you need to have them clinging round
your neck?' He was speaking fast, his mouth contemptuous.

She moved to the door to open it and Steve
reached it at the same time. His hand clamped down
on her wrist and pulled her hand away from the
door handle. Then his hand ran up her bare arm,

softly caressing the warm golden skin, making the tiny bright hairs on her flesh prickle with response.

'Haven't you done enough to me?' That was a cry from the heart, but the only reply it got was a slow, sensual smile which answered without the need for words.

'I hate you,' she whispered, her eyes on the floor because she dared not look at him. At close quarters the masculine strength of his lean body had a hypnotic effect on her. She wanted to lean forward and let her whole weight rest on that broad chest. She was tired of running, tired of fighting. Only the memory of his cruelty kept her from caving in like a fool.

'Do you?' She was not looking at him, but she heard the smile in his voice and she resented his confidence. He was fondling her shoulder now, his long fingers pressing into her flesh, tracing the slope of the bone. She couldn't move. She stood there, her head bent in a defensive weakness, her neck tingling as his fingers moved towards it. She had to stop him; she had to fight the need inside herself.

'Is Lister your lover?' He asked the question so softly, so smoothly, his voice careful.

Silently she shook her head, suppressing the sigh which wrenched her. His hand had reached her throat now. It curved round it possessively and his fingers moved up into her full, cloudy hair. She heard his breathing change, quicken.

Abruptly she wrenched herself away and faced him, her head up now, her green eyes defiant and frightened.

'I told you,' she muttered wearily. 'Never again.'

The sensual feeling went out of his face. His mouth straightened into that hard, cold line she recognised only too clearly. 'Yes,' he told her, 'you will. I won't let you go. Until I'm tired of you I am going to keep you.'

'I got away from you once. I'll get away from you again,' she said with more confidence than she felt.

He shook his head, the blue eyes enigmatic now, their expression hidden from her by the droop of his eyelids. 'You know better than to try to run again. You wouldn't get five yards.'

'Are you having me watched?' she burst out, her voice shaking.

He took in her anxiety and fear with sardonic eyes, smiling. 'What do you think? I learnt my lesson when you bolted last time. You aren't getting away from me again.'

She looked at him with hatred. 'You're mad! What can you possibly get out of it? You hate me, but you won't leave me alone.'

He moved closer again, cruelty in every line of his face. 'I'll leave you alone when I'm satisfied, and until then you're going to pay over and over again for what you did to me.' The blue eyes flashed. 'How do you think I felt when that policeman told me that my wife had crashed on her way to a love-nest with her lover? If Harrison hadn't been dead already I'd have had to kill him. I was crazy about you, it had never entered my head that you could be two-timing me. And all those months the two of you had been laughing at me behind my back. How many times did you fly off with him on some pretext of working? Do you think I didn't sit and think about those weekends when I was away and you and Harrison were free to go to bed without being afraid I'd walk in and catch you at it?'

Lisa shrank back against the door, shivering, seeing the aroused bitterness in his face, the ice in the blue eyes. 'It isn't true!'

'No?' The black brows curved upward in derisive sarcasm. 'I suppose I imagined those love letters of his?'

She looked away, her face burning. Denny had bombarded her with passionate, pleading letters during the last months. She had burnt some of them, but foolishly she had just thrust others into a drawer, partly out of a sense of guilt over Denny, a wrung sensation of pity for him. The wildness of his love for her had made her feel sick. She had never even realised what was building up in him until it was too late. It was then that she should have stopped seeing him, but she had owed him so much. Denny had loaded her with obligations right from the start. It was not easy to walk out on someone who has done so much for you.

'Well?' Steve insisted thickly. 'Tell me I dreamt those.'

'No,' she whispered. 'Denny loved me, I can't deny that. What could I do? You know how highly strung he was—he was an artist, brilliant, but unstable. Everything he did was extreme. He was generous and selfless, but he always went over the top in everything he did. I know I should have stopped seeing him when I realised how he felt, but how could I? I was fond of him and I felt sorry for him. I didn't know what to do.'

'You could have told me,' Steve said through his teeth, staring down at her. 'You never breathed a word to me. You let me go on thinking the two of you were brother and sister.'

'We were,' she cried miserably, 'once. Then it changed—Denny changed.' She looked at him pleadingly. 'I didn't, Steve. I never loved Denny like that, I swear it!'

Steve's face had a hard rage in it. 'You just gave yourself to him out of pity,' he said in icy contempt. 'He whined and begged until you gave in, did he? My God, when I read some of those letters I almost threw up. He tried to use every lever he had, didn't he? He had no self-respect. There was nothing too low for him to use if he thought it would get him what he wanted, and in the end it did, didn't it?'

She shook her head wildly. 'No, no, no.'

'Even if that were true,' Steve said fiercely, 'you had let him get too close. You gave him too much that belonged to me. You had no business letting another man encroach on my territory. I thought you just worked well together. It never entered my head that all this was going on under the surface. I don't blame you for the fact that he fell for you, but I do blame you for letting him write to you like that, for going on working with him, spending so much time with him. Even if it was all innocent on the physical level, which I don't believe, you were being unfaithful to me, whether you accept that or not, every time you got one of those letters and didn't show it to me.'

There was too much truth in that for her to be able to deny it. She had thought the same herself ever since. She should have stopped working with Denny. She should have told Steve what was going on between them. She hadn't. She had hidden it from Steve. Like those letters, she had pushed it into the back of a closed drawer. But you can never do that with people. They misunderstand. She had tried being gentle and understanding with Denny, tried to show him she could never care for him in that way while letting him see she was fond of him, as she always had been. Denny had read something quite different into her actions.

'Harrison tried to steal you from me,' said Steve in a voice which dropped the words out like icicles, clear and hard and cold. 'And you let him do it. Whatever your reasons, you let him take over parts of your life which were mine. Every moment you spent with him once you knew he loved you was a moment stolen from me.' She caught the dark flicker in his face and instinctively moved back, but she was too late. There was nowhere to run to—she found herself with her back quite literally to the wall and Steve's long hard body crushing her, his hands moulding her face between them, tilting it so that he could look down into the frightened green eyes.

'I want it all back,' he said huskily. 'Nobody steals anything from me. You'll pay back every moment of the hours you gave to him, and I want it repaid with interest.'

His mouth came down in a forceful, punitive exploration, bruising her lips apart, wringing response out of her, his lips awakening every instinct in her flesh. She could not back away or evade because he held her head between those long hands, his fingers gripping her cheekbones like a vice. His body moved against her in a restless eagerness, the hard thighs forced down on her. For a second she felt the hot tide rising inside her and then she cut it off with a deliberate intention. Not this time, she thought. She was not even going to fight. It was her new weapon, a static resistance which did not struggle yet which did not yield an inch. She lay in his arms with the hungry pressure of his body on hers, and she was as cold as ice.

In the end Steve slowly drew back, lifting his head and looking at her with a visible surprise and anger.

'Not any more,' she told him in a flat, calm voice.

'You want me,' he broke out hoarsely, dark red burning in his face. 'You always have. You never wanted Harrison—you just threw yourself to him to stop the little cur whining. But you want me—we proved that, didn't we? Whatever I did or said to you I could always have you.'

'Not any more,' she repeated. 'I'm a burnt-out case, Steve. I just don't care. It's over.'

He had pushed her too far and under that pressure she had managed to cut herself off from him. The room grew chill with a marrow-freezing cold which came from inside herself. However badly he had treated her, her love for him had been a warmth, a human connection which linked her with life. She was not sure when she had begun to withdraw from that; perhaps when they were in Florida, that first week in hell, when Steve had shown her a side of his nature that appalled her. The ruthless torturer who had watched her suffer and smiled was not a man she would ever want to live with again. She had run because she had had enough pain, but she had not stopped loving him then. When she saw him again she had felt the same confused desire he had delighted in arousing in her in Florida, but now she just felt cold and tired and indifferent.

She leaned against the wall and Steve's narrowed blue eyes surveyed her, reading the pale weary face and empty green eyes.

He straightened and released her, stepping back. 'What happened was as much destructive for me as it was for you,' he said in a deep angry voice. 'You weren't the only one who went through hell. Hasn't that ever occurred to you? I was going out of my mind.'

'That's no excuse for what you did.'

'I'm not making excuses!' The lithe body was stiff, his eyes burning with feeling. 'I'm a human being. If someone hurts me, I hurt back.'

She bent her head, shivering. 'I never meant to hurt you. It was the last thing I wanted to do. I hate hurting people.' Why else had she let Denny go on hoping when it was hopeless? Pity was destructive, it was folly. She raised her eyes and stared at him coldly. 'But you deliberately set out to hurt me. You wanted to smash me into little pieces.'

His features blazed with conflicting emotions;

anger, passion, pain, and for a moment he stood there staring at her fixedly, his lips moving but no words emerging.

Then he pulled open the door and left without a word, slamming it after him so that the windows shook and Lisa trembled, her hands covering her white face.

She sat down in a chair and stared at the wall unseeingly. Her hands were so cold. She rubbed them together, her teeth chattering.

She had first met Denny when she was eighteen. She had just left school in England and had been visiting her mother in New York. Her father had died when she was sixteen. Lisa had been shocked and unhappy and her depression had deepened when, just a year later, her mother had remarried an American she had met in London. Lisa elected to stay in England and finish her education. Her mother flew off with her new husband, leaving Lisa to stay with an aunt while she completed her schooling. When that was ended, Lisa flew to the States to stay with her mother and stepfather while she decided what to do.

She met Denny in a restaurant. He quite literally picked her up after she had tripped over a step. When he told her he was a photographer and insisted that she would be a natural for a career in modelling, Lisa's common sense had warned her that it was just a line he was selling her.

She had been wrong. Denny was just what he had claimed to be—a well-known and successful photographer. Lisa's mother had been very excited at the opportunity her daughter had been given. Even if Lisa had not wanted to take up that career, her mother would have tried to press her to agree.

Denny was a thin, energetic man of thirty with pale dusty hair and intense light eyes. He was a slave-driver, showing no signs of tiring even when Lisa's whole body ached as if she had been running in a marathon, and his temper never slipped when she was on the point of screaming like a fishwife. He would repeat an action over and over again for hour after hour. He demanded a disciplined response, selfless work and untiring obedience.

She came to admire his flair, his intuition, his brilliance, and the debt she owed him for what he did for her career grew as she climbed up the ladder to the success he had promised her.

'You've got to learn to project,' he told her. 'We're selling you, darling, and we have to make the product irrisistible. I'll do my side, but that's half the problem. You've got all the natural ingredients, you have to learn to sell them.'

Denny had been more than a task-master, though. He had been her protection. Lisa had not needed to tell Denny that she was alarmed by the avidity with which men watched her. The interest her body aroused disturbed her. At that time Denny gave her the sexless admiration of the artist. It was a feeling which did not include the greed to possess. Denny looked and appreciated without needing to snatch.

Their first big break came with a lingerie advertisement. Denny photographed her in delicate white lace bra and panties, lying on a black silk bed, her eyes half-closed in the languorous gaze of a woman who is awaking from love; her lips parted slightly, her lower lip full and throbbing, as though bruised by kisses, her hand thrust negligently into the brilliant cloud of hair spilling over the pillows.

The company whose products they were selling were ecstatic. They immediately signed for a full-scale campaign using Lisa, and very soon she found herself in heavy demand by clients who saw that by linking their products with her sensuous body and smouldering green eyes they could increase sales. Denny was able to command enormous fees for her and Lisa had been overwhelmed with relief because for months she had lived by Denny's generosity and she felt easier now that she no longer owed him the price of everything she wore, everything she ate.

Denny had been successful in the past, but Lisa was the most successful model he had ever had. He had guessed she would be—he had let that intuition of his guide him and he had been proved right.

She met Steve Crawford when she did a television commercial for his company. Denny had given her a breakdown on him beforehand. 'He's tough and rich and clever and he likes women. If he makes a pass, just play it cool. I'll be around.'

Denny had stayed beside her when Steve turned those wickedly amused blue eyes on her, and she had been grateful for his presence because within minutes of meeting Steve she felt a warning flicker of excitement deep inside her.

Steve had smiled and watched her and said very little. Denny wasn't there when he arrived at her apartment two days later. Lisa told herself it was madness to go out with Steve Crawford, but somehow that was just what she did. He tried to make love to her that first evening and she had firmly held him off. Denny had to go to Chicago to visit a friend during the following week. While he was away she saw Steve every day. She still kept him at arm's length, but it got more difficult every time. She knew it was only a matter of time. She was in love with him within a week of that first meeting and all her carefully thought out decisions about not getting dragged into an affair had dissolved to nothing the first time he kissed her.

In fact, it never happened, because Steve's first urgent pressure suddenly changed. Later, she knew he changed because he discovered he was in love with her. At the time she had been confused, disturbed, afraid she had lost him.

He proposed to her six weeks after their first meeting and she accepted.

He was a very busy man and, since she kept up her career, they spent a good deal of time apart, necessarily, but it had been a deeply happy marriage. They both liked the same things and they were passionate lovers. Steve slightly despised Denny. The powerful, dominating masculinity Steve possessed totally obliterated Denny's slight physical presence, and the highly strung intensity of the artist which Denny had used to such brilliant effect in his job became a positive disadvantage in opposition to Steve's tough arrogance.

It was probably from her marriage that Denny's

alteration dated, Lisa saw later. While they worked together as a pair against the world, Denny continued to see her as his creation: the woman he had fashioned and breathed into life.

Her marriage shattered him. He had argued, pleaded, shouted, even gone to the point of tears. In all other areas of her life Lisa had permitted him to make the decisions, but this was different. She loved Steve and nothing was allowed to stand in her way.

When Denny first told her he loved her, she had been too shaken to know what to do. She should have walked away from him then, but old loyalty held her, and from then on it got worse. The letters started, the late night phone calls, the pleading and accusations, the constant attempt to touch her.

Thinking back later she saw that Denny's vision of her as the perfect woman, his living, breathing work of art, had given him the feeling that he owned her. She belonged to him. When she married Steve she deserted him, betrayed him, and Denny was frantic to re-possess what he saw as his creation.

It wasn't so bad when they were working. Denny lapsed into his usual absorbed fascination with the technique of filming her. He was a genius, in his way. Lisa's career had not halted when she married Steve. She had gone on working and making a great deal of money. Steve had not asked her to stop; he had accepted that she had her career, as he had his, and having seen her with Denny in the weeks before their marriage it had never crossed Steve's mind, any

more than it had hers, that Denny felt anything for
her but the pride of professional achievement.

She hid it all from Steve because she knew that if
she told him he would make her stop working with
Denny, and by then she was Denny's work, his life,
his whole existence. Everything in Denny's life was
bound up with her. Once everything in her life had
been bound up with Denny. Steve's arrival had ended
that. She had been the one who walked out on Denny
in an emotional sense. She could not bring herself to
walk out altogether. It would hurt Denny too much.

So she had slid down that slippery slope of pity
and guilt and confusion until the car crash and
Denny's death.

What else could she have done? Steve would say
she should have been clear-sighted and ruthless
enough to cut Denny out of her life.

Maybe she should have done. Maybe now she
would, if the same circumstances occurred. Or would
she?

People were emotional parasites. You bumped
into them in some haphazard collision and the next
thing you knew they were growing all round you,
clinging with thin tenacious little tentacles, and they
were absorbing your life in order to enrich their own.

When she walked into Wrights she knew nothing of the people there, but they had immediately
picked up her inner strengths, and Evan and Anna
had seen her at once as a strong support for Jon.
Anna was blatant in her attempt to foist her brother
on to Lisa. Evan, for all his impatience with Jon,
had used Lisa to shore him up. Jon himself was

ready to use her as a buffer between himself and Evan.

She should go now before things got more difficult. Steve was cynically exploiting her dislike of hurting people. The contract he was offering Wrights had only one purpose—to force her back to him. All she had to do was go and the weapon would be useless to him. But if she did go there would be other consequences: Evan would be furious with Jon and Anna would be furious with Evan.

Is that my business? she asked herself. Let them get on with it. They're not my problem. They're three adults and it's time they sorted out the mess they've made of Jon's life. Jon should have the guts to see what was happening and go.

If she loved Jon it would be understandable, but all she felt for him, as it had been with Denny, was pity and affection, a disastrous combination, and she should know better than to let it happen all over again. Jon wasn't Denny, of course. He lacked Denny's unstable intensity. He was just weak, helpless, in need of moral bolstering.

She stood up, her face pale and stiff. I must get out of the whole mess, she told herself. I must!

CHAPTER FIVE

She could not stay in the flat; the room was echoing with the sound of Steve's embittered voice and she had to get out. She took off her apron and flung it down, grabbed a jacket and went out to the shops, where she spent a long time wandering vaguely around buying a lot of things she did not want. When she got back, Magda was singing brightly as she ironed in the living-room.

'You had a phone call,' she said with excitement, breaking off to stare at Lisa's pale face. 'You'll never guess who!'

Couldn't I? Lisa thought, going into the tiny kitchen. Magda followed her, asking: 'Don't you want to know who it was? He didn't actually say, but I recognised the voice—nobody else talks like that. On the phone he sounds even sexier, like a hungry tiger.'

She paused as Lisa began to unpack her useless purchases. 'What on earth have you bought that for?' She picked up one of them. 'Smoked cheese? You hate it. Are you planning a party? Any chocolate ants?'

Lisa was forced to laugh at that. They had eaten those monstrous things at a party and not known what they were until their host laughingly told them, when they had both felt sick. The crunchy golden things Magda had declared so delicious, they were gleefully informed, had been crystallised bees. That had been a party to forget.

Magda put down the cheese. 'Anyway, it was Steve Crawford. I told him you'd gone out, but he sounded as though he didn't believe that. He said he'd pick you up at twelve.' She glanced at her watch. 'It's nearly that now, you'd better hurry.' A wry resignation filled her face. 'I knew it was too good to be true that he had an eye on me when you were around.'

'I'm not going,' Lisa said flatly, turning to put some of her packages into the fridge.

'You're kidding!' Magda gazed, open-mouthed. 'You're turning down lunch with him? Are you out of your mind? I'd jump at the chance.'

'Jump, then,' said Lisa in dry tones as she walked out of the room. Magda followed her to her bedroom and watched as Lisa stripped off her shirt and jeans.

'Don't you fancy him? Honestly?'

'I'm going to have a bath,' Lisa said. 'When he comes tell him I'm out.'

She was glad to close the bathroom door on Magda's puzzled, incredulous eyes. She ran the water and saturated it in fragrance. Lying back with closed eyes she let the warmth and perfume seep into her. The room was filled with steam. She didn't think of anything. She was empty, a husk.

Stepping out of the bath at last, she wrapped herself in an enormous white towel. In the mirror she saw her face flushed now from the bath, her green eyes dilated, her hair pinned up on top of her head and giving her bare neck a defenceless curve. Grimacing, she turned and listened at the door. There wasn't a sound. If Steve had come, he must have gone again.

She opened the door and walked to her bedroom, leaving little wet footprints on the grey carpet. For a moment she didn't notice him and then she stopped, shaking. He was lying on her bed with his

hands behind his head and the blue eyes riveted on
her.

She gathered the last of her strength and said
flatly: 'If you don't get out of here I'll scream the
place down.' Why on earth had Magda let him come
in here? How could she?

He slid his long legs off the bed. She instinctively
took a step backward, but she was so weary that her
reflexes were too slow. Steve had reached her before
she got out of the room. He caught her shoulders,
his hands warm on her damp flesh, and looked down
at her with those half-closed sensual eyes.

Her whole body began to tremble. She gripped
the towel, her arms crossed across her breast in a
timeless gesture of female defence, and tried to stare
him out.

He didn't move, watching her, his eyes probing
her weak defences, and she looked away because if
she let him he would read all the aching need he was
arousing in her. Heat was stinging along her veins
and she was fiercely conscious of the fact that she
was naked under the towel and that Steve knew it.

She heard the thick, stifled sound he made and
turned to look at him nervously. He pulled her towards him with his eyes fixed on her mouth. The kiss
was different, this time, though. It was gentle and
persuasive, coaxing her to respond, and she knew he
was changing his tactics because of her earlier ob-
duracy.

'Get dressed,' he muttered as he lifted his head.
'We're having lunch at one.'

She shook her head. 'I told you ...'

'And I told you,' Steve informed her drily, 'I'm giving you a choice, my darling. Either you come out to lunch or I take off that towel and we spend an enjoyable hour in here.'

She flushed to her hairline. 'Don't you think Magda might be rather curious about what we were doing?'

His eyes mocked her. 'Your delightful flatmate has gone off to lunch herself.'

Lisa remembered then that Magda had mentioned a lunch date with one of her casual boy-friends. She should have remembered that. Steve had persuaded Magda to leave him alone in the flat and then he had come in here and waited.

He read her irritation and laughed softly. 'I'm sure I don't need to tell you what I'd prefer to do,' he whispered, his hands dropping to the place where she had tucked the towel together across her breasts.

She pushed his hands away. 'No!'

'Get dressed, then,' he said, grinning. 'I'll wait outside. And if you try to lock yourself in, remember, I've no compunction about breaking down doors.'

'Or people,' she retorted bitterly.

His eyes flicked at her. 'Can't we have a truce for a few hours, Lisa? You look tired.' There was a gentleness in his face as he spoke, a trace of the man she had once loved passionately. 'I thought we might have a leisurely lunch and then you can show me Kew Gardens or the Tower of London.'

She felt a tremor in her throat as she saw him walk out. Had he softened? It was dangerous to hope, but she couldn't help it. Sighing, she turned and glanced through her clothes in search of something to wear. She took down a classic white silk shirt and chose a black pencil skirt to go with it. They were unexciting but elegant and wouldn't give Steve any ideas.

It took her nearly half an hour and when she joined him he threw down the book of nineteenth century verse he had been skimming through and ran a comprehensive glance over her, his mouth wry.

'Elegant,' he mocked. 'I shan't have to fight off the ravening hordes today, shall I?' He knew that she had been underplaying her looks when she chose to wear that outfit. There wasn't much she could do about her figure. Denny had not needed to teach her how to move—she had been born with that swaying rhythm in her bones. It was something to do with her height, which was tall for a girl, and her perfect physical proportions, although she had often complained to Denny that she was too tall and too thin. Other girls she worked with had little obsessions of that kind. Some thought themselves too wide either in the bust or the hips; others moaned continually about their colouring or their large feet.

They lunched beside the river at a table near the window. The sound of the lapping water gave a peaceful air to the busy restaurant. Lisa had fresh grapefruit juice followed by a salad. Steve had pâté, which he had usually had in the past, and a steak. They did not talk much as they ate. Steve refilled her wine glass and watched her across the table with teasing blue eyes.

He kept his conversation light and impersonal. Gradually the wine slackened the tension inside Lisa's body and she felt colour coming back into her face.

A slim blonde in a skin-tight pair of leopardskin pants sauntered past and gave Steve a sideways glance which he returned with amused interest.

Lisa looked down at her melting sorbet and poked her spoon at it petulantly. When she looked up again, the blue eyes were watching her and she had to glance away before he saw the expression in her own eyes.

Before he met her, Steve had had other women. At their first meeting he had taken one look at her and decided he wanted her, proceeding with typical assurance to reach out to take what he wanted. Her resistance had surprised him. Her career had never depended on any sexual bargaining, but it was not unusual in that world for ambitious girls to use their bodies as collateral. Steve had imagined that she would be an easy conquest and it had taken her some time to disillusion him. Having seen the hardening effect of that sort of life on other girls, Lisa had determined not to have it happen to her, and Denny's championship of her had protected her from that.

Steve's previous relationships had all been temporary and without depth. Lisa told herself at the time that it did not matter, but she had never quite been able to silence a nagging jealousy, particularly if she saw him talking to an attractive woman and became aware that at some time in the past they had had an affair.

Steve had never been unfaithful to her; that had been one of the things that had embittered him after Denny's death. 'Do you think I couldn't have cheated on you?' he had asked fiercely. 'Do you think I haven't been offered the chance time and time again? And I was fool enough to turn down offers without even thinking about it.' His blue eyes had burnt with rage as he stared at her. 'Not any more, sweetheart.'

During those dreadful weeks he had been too obsessed with hurting her and forcing her to a continual sexual humiliation to carry out his implied threat of infidelity in turn, but she couldn't imagine that during the past year Steve had been without consolation.

They were both silent as they drank their coffee. Steve paid the bill and guided her out of the restaurant, his arm just behind her waist, not touching her, yet there so that she felt the warmth of his body close behind her own.

'Kew, then?' he asked, his hands on the wheel of his car.

'If you like.' She was faintly drowsy after the wine, her green eyes too brilliant in her flushed face.

He turned his head to look at her, then smiled, his eyes teasing again. His long fingers reached out and undid the top button of her shirt, spreading the collar open to reveal her smooth brown throat.

The feel of those fingers moving against her skin sent a wave of heated desire through her. She closed her eyes, breathing harshly, and his hand came up to touch her cheek, trail over the warm skin, his fingertips caressing. He ran the fingers along the line of her mouth and her lips parted on a sigh.

Then he had withdrawn his hand and she heard the ignition catch, the throb of the engine. She lay there with shut eyes, breathing like someone who has just climbed a mountain. Her heart was beating so fast she felt sick.

Was this a new version of his special brand of torture? Was he playing with her like a cat with a mouse, waiting until she betrayed herself into his hands again? They had spent several hours together without one single angry word, one single bitter look from him. Steve had to be lulling her into a false sense of security. Only this morning he had been as cruel as ever, telling her coldly that she was going to pay for what she had done to him. Now he was whistling as he drove, his profile relaxed, the hard mouth half-smiling.

She would be insane to let him trap her again. Last time she had almost gone mad; this time he would finish the process.

When they got to Kew Steve made her walk around with him to inspect the most famous parts of the botanical gardens: the red pagoda which had stood in surprising splendour in that English setting for years, amusing schoolchildren and amazing foreigners, the giant redwoods which dwarfed the English trees around them, the perfect lawns and flowerbeds which spread on all sides, and lastly the glasshouses whose tropical heat sheltered exotic inter-lopers from overseas.

Steve regarded the Venus Flytrap with a wry, ironic little smile and turned his eyes to Lisa, his brows lifting. She flushed, needing no words to explain the meaning of that derisive but silent comment. A party being shown round by a guide watched in revolted fascination as the man delicately stroked the plant with a pencil which he withdrew before the closing serrated edges could engulf it.

Steve laughed under his breath and Lisa walked away, her back stiff with temper.

He caught her up. 'No sense of humour, that's your problem,' he whispered.

'I didn't think it was funny!'

'No,' he agreed, laughing.

They stood before an incredible collection of fleshy, speckled orchids. 'Horrible things,' Lisa said defensively, glaring at Steve. If he said they reminded him of her she would hit him.

He didn't, however. His mouth twisted and he said coolly: 'No, they're not your flower.'

'What is?' she asked, half curious, half relieved.

He lowered his lashes and wore a curious little smile. 'My love is like a red, red rose,' he said with mocking derision, and she did not know whether to slap him or burst into tears. He went on teasingly, 'You should have been a gypsy in a tiered skirt with a red rose between your teeth. You have that half-tamed look. I'm surprised Harrison didn't use that image.'

She was surprised that he should mention Denny with such calm indifference. For so long the name could make Steve spit like a savage tiger, his lips bared in a snarl.

His lashes lifted and his blue eyes were brilliant.

'Not that you look like a gypsy today—more the chic career woman. I don't know why Wright doesn't give you Lister's job. You could do it with one hand behind your back, whereas Lister hasn't got a snowball's chance in hell of making a name for himself. The man's a fumbling idiot. Does he always drink like that?'

She turned and walked away. 'Only when he's scared stiff,' she threw over her shoulder. 'You terrified him. Evan terrifies him.'

'He's in the wrong job.'

'He knows that,' Lisa said angrily.

'Then why doesn't he clear out?'

'It isn't that easy.' She paused in the bright afternoon sunlight to look at him impatiently. 'It never is, Steve. I know people like you think it's always a straightforward business, but life is often more complicated than you'll ever realise.'

'What's complicated about Lister's life?' He sounded as though he wanted to know and she hesitated because Steve used every morsel of information he got hold of, and although she could not see how he could use what she told him about Jon and Anna she still felt rather dubious about telling him.

He searched her hesitant face, his brows drawing together. 'Are you involved in this?' The hardness came back and his blue eyes went icy. 'Is he in love with you?'

She sighed. 'No. Jon wouldn't know how. He has a very low sex drive and life is already too worrying for him to want any further complications.'

'So what's bugging him?' Steve asked curtly.

She bit her lip and shrugged. Steve listened as she told him about Anna and Evan, explained Anna's insistence that Jon should rise in the advertising business, Jon's misery and inability to cope.

'As I thought,' Steve commented drily when she had finished, 'another of your lame ducks. So he doesn't fancy you?'

She lifted her head in sudden defiance, angry with him because he dismissed Jon with such cavalier contempt. 'I didn't say that. Jon thinks I'd make the perfect wife for a rising young executive.'

'*Does* he?' Steve murmured in sardonic emphasis. 'And does dear sister Anna think so too?'

'Actually, she does,' said Lisa, reckless because he was watching her with those hard blue eyes and she didn't like the way he was doing it.

'Then it's time we told them you aren't free,' Steve observed softly.

'But I am free,' Lisa flung, flushed and excited. 'Free of you. I belong to myself.'

'Do you?' He was watching her with that crooked little smile and she couldn't tell what effect her defiance was having on him.

'Yes, I do,' she said clearly. 'When you get back to the States you can start divorce proceedings. I won't need any alimony. I wouldn't touch a penny of your money.'

Some tourists wandering past eyed her, guessing no doubt from her flushed face and angry eyes that there was a row going on right under their noses.

'And if I divorced you, what then?' Steve enquired as though he were merely curious. 'You'd marry Lister?'

She shrugged, feeling the excited heat draining out of her at his tone. 'I might.'

'Like hell,' he sneered. 'Lister would run a mile. You're an explosive mixture, my darling, and the poor idiot knows he couldn't handle you. I watched the pair of you when I had dinner at Wrights—Lister looked at you as though you might blow up in his face. You're too passionate for an anaemic fool like that—he's afraid you'd eat him up like the Venus Flytrap. I know his type. Women have dominated him all his life and he's scared stiff of them. You say his sister loves him but she also pushes him around. No, Lister is a born bachelor, or a man destined to marry someone like his sister who won't demand too much of him but will mother him and bully him all his life.'

Steve had put into words her own feelings about Jon, but it annoyed her. She had been deliberately teasing him and he had refused to rise to the bait. She moved away and he walked beside her, eyeing her with amusement.

'You like to live dangerously, don't you?' he asked.

She pretended innocence. 'What?'

'You know what I mean.'

She did know, and she also knew why she had deliberately teased him like that. Seeing that blonde eyeing him in the restaurant she had begun to imagine exactly what Steve had been up to in the past year, and she was jealous.

'You know I won't give you a divorce,' he drawled.

'I can get detectives too, you know,' she flared. 'I've no doubt they'd give me some pretty useful evidence if they asked around New York.'

He laughed under his breath. 'So that's it!'

She didn't answer, walking faster. He kept pace with her without difficulty, his long strides leisurely.

'You ran out on me,' he observed. 'What do you expect? Celibacy has never had much appeal for me and I had no problems finding willing volunteers.'

She had known it must be the case, but she felt her throat closing up in rage and jealousy as she listened. They had reached the car. Steve unlocked it and she took her seat, averting her face as he climbed into the driver's seat.

He didn't start the car. He sat there watching her, his fingers drumming on the wheel. After a silence he asked softly: 'Jealous, Lisa?'

She didn't answer, the curve of her cheek hiding her expression from him.

'Apart from Lister has there been anyone for you?' he asked when he realised she had no intention of answering.

'That's my business,' she said tightly.

He put a hand under her chin and wrenched her head round. Her eyes flared bitterly at him, green as grass.

'Has there?' he asked insistently.

'Dozens,' she snapped.

He bent forward suddenly before she could move away. His mouth crushed down on hers demandingly, hurting and pleasing her. She put her hands on his chest to push him away, but the movement was never carried through. Her hands flattened against him, feeling the warmth of his body under her palms, hearing the beat of his heart as he forced back her head and deepened the kiss to a hot, insistent possession. Slowly her hands moved up to his shoulders and then she was clinging to him, kissing him back, murmuring hoarsely as her hands stroked his hair and neck.

When he finally released her she was trembling and Steve was darkly flushed. He turned and started the car without a word, while Lisa stared out of the window, biting her lower lip. It had been a long, long time since Steve had kissed her like that, with passion but without a desire to hurt. That had been an echo of their first months together when love had been paramount in their relationship, a shared exploration of their minds and bodies which had deepened their feelings for each other day after day.

He drove her back to her flat and switched off the engine. She sat there, staring at the quiet road. Steve turned and looked at her.

'Come back to my flat,' he said huskily.

Had he just taken her there she might well have gone in and yielded without a struggle, but he had given her a chance to think, and she shook her head slowly.

'Why not?' he asked. 'You want it as much as I do—don't tell me you don't. Do you think I couldn't feel it?'

'I shall never come back to you until you believe me when I say Denny was never my lover.' Lisa had told herself that when she ran from him. She could never again allow him to treat her the way he had treated her during those terrible weeks after the crash. Only a masochist could put up with such treatment.

Steve studied her as though she were a strange specimen in a zoo, his eyes cold. 'We'll see,' he murmured in a remote voice.

She got out and walked down to the flat. Before she reached the front door he had zoomed away. Magda had not returned and the flat was empty and cold. Lisa did some more housework and then settled down for the evening in front of the television. She was in bed before Magda came home. She heard her go to bed and she lay awake for hours afterwards arguing with herself. Steve had not been the same today. At times he had been the man she had first met and fallen in love with—now and then he had become cold, but for most of the time they spent together he had been charming. She couldn't make up her mind whether or not this was merely some deeplaid plot to trick her into trusting him and going back to the States. If she gave in to her own desire for him and went back to him she might find herself back in that bitter trap from which she had fled a year ago.

She had evaded him so far, but she did not know how much of Steve's concentrated technique she could take before she gave in and let him take what he wanted.

On the Sunday morning Anna rang to ask her over to lunch. 'I want to talk to you.'

No prizes for guessing what she wanted to talk about, Lisa thought, and was proved entirely right. Evan was in a jovial mood, heavily humorous with his sons and getting as good as he gave, teasing Lisa about her heavy-eyed look this morning and asking who had kept her out until all hours. 'Our American friend, I wonder?' he asked innocently, and Anna looked furious.

'You seem to forget, Lisa is Jon's girl,' she snapped.

Evan glanced at her with a wry face. 'You've got to be kidding!' Apart from Evan's desire to use her to lure Steve Crawford into the firm's grip, Evan also saw Jon as a sexual joke. Evan had a dynamic sexual energy, for all that it was turned entirely upon his wife, and he did not have any illusions about his brother-in-law's lack of energy in that direction.

Anna scowled but said nothing. The boys dragged their father off to play table tennis and when they were alone Anna settled down to her purpose for having Lisa to lunch.

'Evan is pleased with Jon over these ideas of his,' she told her. 'Are they really his?' She probed Lisa's face sharply.

'Yes.' That was basically true, although Lisa had improved on them a little.

Anna relaxed. 'Maybe he's getting it at last. I always thought Evan was too hard on him. Jon's capable of much more than Evan will admit.'

Far more talented than Anna could recognise, Lisa thought, because Anna ignored Jon's real qualities and tried to make him reproduce those of her husband.

'Since you joined the firm, Jon's done much better,' Anna told her with satisfaction. 'I've always said that what Jon needs is a woman behind him.'

Evan said Jon needed a boot behind him, and Evan made sure he got it, but both of them read the situation wrongly. All Jon needed to do was to get out of a job he was incapable of doing and find a job which he could do.

Lisa did not comment on Anna's remarks and Anna happily went on to say, 'I must admit I shall feel much happier if Jon is doing well. This is turning out to be a difficult pregnancy.'

Lisa sat up in alarm. 'How do you mean?'

Anna looked at him and smiled. 'Don't tell Evan—I haven't mentioned it to him because he'll only fuss and fume and make things worse.'

'What's wrong?' Lisa asked, staring at her.

'They aren't sure,' said Anna. 'I've got to have some tests. They think the baby isn't growing properly and they want me to have some total rest in the hospital for a month or so. They think I'm overdoing things at home and if I rest the baby will start growing properly.'

Lisa was dismayed. 'I'm so sorry, Anna,' she said, forehead wrinkling. 'Can I help? Would you like me to look after the boys?'

'Catherine is going to do that,' Anna told her. 'But first I've got to break the news to Evan, and you know what will happen. He'll hit the roof and stamp about in one of his rages. I'm waiting until the last moment to tell him, then I can get out before he blows up.'

Evan would be angry, Lisa agreed; he always was when he was alarmed. He would be petrified when he knew there was some sort of problem with this baby and he would turn his fear into violent rage because that was the only way he knew of handling it.

'You'll calm him down for me, won't you?' Anna said cheerfully. 'He trusts you. Make him see it isn't the end of the world. And keep him away from Jon's throat. I'm so relieved to be leaving Jon in your capable hands. I'll be able to rest much more safely knowing Jon won't be entirely at Evan's mercy.'

Why does this happen to me? Lisa thought. Why don't I just tell her: sorry, but your brother is your problem? She looked at Anna's pleading face and knew she couldn't. Anna and her baby had to have that rest.

'Don't worry,' she said with forced brightness. 'I'll keep Evan away from Jon and I'll nurse this deal.'

Anna gave a wide, happy smile and her hands folded in that characteristic gesture of maternity over her lap. 'Thank you,' she said.

CHAPTER SIX

EVAN stood aggressively in the centre of the room with his large hands on his hips. 'They could be hiding the truth from us! Doctors never tell you what they really think.' His skin was flushed, his eyes filled with anger and anxiety. 'Why didn't she tell me? Why spring it on me suddenly like that? Catherine knew, you knew. What am I—some sort of ogre?'

'If you bellowed at her like this, yes!' Lisa told him, keeping her eyes on his taut face. 'The last thing Anna needs just now is an irate husband. It isn't her fault that this has happened. Poor girl, she needs to be cherished, not bullied.'

'Bullied?' Evan's voice roared. 'Me?'

'Yes, you,' she mocked him, half smiling, amused by his look of indignant amazement.

'I've never bullied Anna in my life,' he protested.

Lisa laughed outright. 'You don't know when you're doing it.'

'Look,' he said in that belligerent, bull-like way, 'I've turned over every stone I knew to keep her happy. God knows how patient I've been. I'd have chucked Jon out on his ear long ago if it hadn't been for Anna.' He paused, his ears reddening. 'I love her,' he muttered in a low, furious voice, then shot Lisa a look daring her to comment or even to admit having heard that.

Gently she said: 'You mustn't worry too much. I don't think there's any real risk to the baby. Anna's been overdoing it, that's all. If she rests and gets lots of peace and quiet, things will proceed normally again. She's a healthy woman. It will be fine, Evan.'

'I hope to God it is,' he muttered, moving to the window and staring out with every muscle in his thick neck clotting in tension. 'I couldn't stand it if anything happened to her.'

'It won't.'

'I wish I had your confidence.'

'These things happen, Evan. It will right itself.'

'I wanted a girl,' he said heavily. 'Now all I want is Anna safe and sound.'

There was a silence. Lisa moved over to touch his sleeve, her face uncertain. She did not say anything. After a moment Evan turned and gave her a grim smile.

'Anyway, about this party!'

Her face altered. Warily, she asked: 'Yes? What about it?'

'I want you to be very nice to Crawford. You were a bit standoffish with him when he had dinner at my house. I'm not asking you to abandon any principles, but I can't rely on Jon to keep the man on the line. You'll have to do it. A few smiles don't cost much.'

'I'm a secretary,' she retorted, 'nothing more. The pay isn't good enough for that.'

Evan thought that was very funny. He roared, the grim lines of his face breaking up, and she was quite relieved to see the wicked glint in those yellow eyes.

'Just be nice,' he said as he rolled out of the room,

still chuckling. Lisa sat down behind her desk and
stared at the door. Jon had been as shaken as Evan
to hear of his sister's problem with the baby. He had,
of course, reacted in a very different way, without
any of Evan's furious anxiety. Jon had merely looked
pale and hagridden—Evan-ridden, she corrected,
smiling. Typically, Evan had turned on Jon as the
only cause of Anna's situation. 'How can she rest
when she keeps worrying about you?'

Evan was jealous of Jon, Lisa realised, staring at
the cloud-fretted sky beyond the window. He knew
his wife spent too much of her time in concern for
her brother, and Evan, who was single-minded in his
love for her, resented that. Maybe that was the root
of the whole problem. If Anna did not keep trying to
make her husband accept her brother, Evan might
scarcely have noticed him at all.

That evening, Magda was infuriatingly obsessed
with the party. She had received a personal invitation from Steve on the phone and had been cock-
a-hoop over it. Lisa had felt a quiver of jealous
irritation as she listened to her friend's excited ex-
clamations.

Magda spent hours getting ready, occupying the
bathroom for so long that Lisa hammered on the
door and shouted: 'Are you alive in there? You
haven't been dragged down the plughole by a ten-
foot spider, have you?'

'Don't!' Magda shrieked. She was petrified of
spiders. If she found one lurking in the bath on
autumn mornings she wouldn't cross the threshold,
shuddering in the door with her eyes fixed on the

hairy black legs as though expecting them to reach
out and get her. Lisa knew the feeling.

When Magda reluctantly emerged in a drenching
cloud of perfume, she swam past Lisa, wrapped in
a towel, saying: 'I have to look my best.'

'If you go like that you'll certainly make an impression on him,' Lisa told her drily.

Magda giggled and slammed into her own room.
Lisa went into the bathroom and looked at herself
in the mirror. She was nervous.

When she had finished getting ready there was still
no sign of Magda. 'I hope it's going to be worth it,'
she muttered to herself. She got out the half bottle
of gin which they kept for visitors and looked at it
in indecision for a moment. She hated the taste of
the stuff, it had such a bitter flavour. But tonight she
needed it. She poured herself a small glass of it and
added orange to help the taste.

Magda arrived belatedly and gaped at her. It was
so rare for Lisa to drink that she was torn between
a comment on that and a dazed comment on the
dress Lisa was wearing. Magda had never seen it before. Lisa had not worn it or shown it to her.

It had been a present from Steve, made for her by
a couturier in New York; white, a straight sheath
from breast to calf, the thin silk undergown moulded
her lovingly and the overgown of white lace rustled
as she walked, slits at the sides giving deliberate
glimpses of her long, smooth legs.

'Where did you get that? When? It must have
cost the earth! How much was it? Where on earth

did you find it?' Magda's questions came too fast for an answer to be given.

It must have cost a fortune, but she had no idea how much Steve had paid for it. 'I like buying my women clothes,' he had told her teasingly. 'Then they can't complain when I rip them off.' The wicked blue eyes had laughed at her and she had laughed back.

'You dare!' she had told him. 'I love it.'

'So do I,' Steve had murmured. 'But I like you better without it.'

That had been the end of that conversation, but despite his threat he had been very careful as he took the dress off, and it was a present which had nothing but happy memories attached to it.

To Magda she only said: 'I've had it for years. It isn't something you can wear that often.'

'I'd wear it every day of my life,' Magda breathed excitedly. She looked at the glass in Lisa's hand. 'What's up with you? You don't often drink.'

'I'm getting into a party mood,' Lisa said recklessly, swallowing the drink. The alcohol circulated in her blood and brought a flush to her face and a stinging awareness to her nerves. She had not dressed like this for months. Her own reflection threw back the familiar, forgotten sensuality, her golden shoulders rising from the low neckline and glimmering smoothly, the soft cloudy hair brushing them as she moved her head.

'He's not going to notice me tonight,' sighed Magda in discontented resignation, staring at her.

Lisa smiled at her. 'Nonsense! You look fantastic.

Green is your colour.' It was true that Magda looked
lively and charming, her eyes cleverly outlined to
deepen their velvety shade.

'Oh, well,' Magda shrugged, 'maybe I'll meet
someone else. A party is always promising.'

Lisa laughed, eyeing her with amusement. Magda
didn't have a chance with Steve, of course, but she
couldn't tell her that or why. It would be wisest for
Magda not to waste her time in hoping.

When Jon picked them up Magda let him in and
Lisa heard her saying: 'Get your sunglasses on,
you're going to need them.'

'What?' Jon sounded impatient and baffled.

He came into the room and stopped dead, his
mouth open. Lisa was winding a silvery shawl around
her shoulders in a graceful movement. She smiled at
him. He was going out of her life and she wasn't
sorry, because she did not want to be involved with
anyone ever again. His awestruck look did nothing
to her. Tonight her real self had surfaced.

She had been living a lie while she was working
at the agency. Her inner light had been deliberately
damped down, her manner offhand and polite. It
hadn't been easy to discard the carefully acquired
tricks which Denny had taught her all those years
ago—the gliding walk, the insinuating sway of the
body, the smouldering gaze which beckoned and yet
rebuked. She could not hide the instinctive movements of her body or alter her features, but she had
worked on the inner mood which the face betrayed,
keeping sexual challenge out of her eyes, out of her
voice. Denny had shown her how to project that

challenge; she had taught herself how to avoid it.

The party was already crowded and noisy when they arrived. Lisa glanced around the room and saw Steve dancing with a small, lively brunette who was winding her arm around his neck in an inviting way.

The way they were dancing made Lisa so angry she had to fight to keep it out of her face. She turned her head to look at Jon and smiled at him. 'Shall we dance?' The smoky invitation made Jon look alarmed. He swallowed. She had never turned that sort of smile, that husky voice, towards him and he was stupefied.

He dumbly moved with her to where people were dancing. Steve's rented flat was large and decorated in a chic, modernistic fashion. People stood around drinking, talking, laughing. Others danced to muted music. Magda had been immediately swallowed into a cheerful group in the centre of which Evan was holding forth, his voice dominating the conversation.

Lisa danced with both hands on Jon's shoulders, her face lifted to his, her eyes half-closed, a lazy tease in the curve of her mouth as she gazed at him. Jon stared back bolt-eyed. He looked like a man who has caught what he imagined to be a tame cat only to find it is a tigress.

Steve was too shrewd, Lisa thought. He had told her that Jon would find her alarming, and judging from Jon's wary expression that was just the impression she was creating in him. It did not matter; she had no designs on Jon. It was for Steve's watching eyes that she moved languidly in Jon's arms, never looking away from his dazed face. She slid her hands along his shoulders and saw him gulp. Suppressing a smile, she decided it was doing him a favour to show him they weren't suited. Jon would never want to get caught with her again, she suspected. She wouldn't need to convince him she was the wrong woman for him after tonight.

One of her hands softly touched his hair. 'It's going to be a great party,' she murmured.

Jon's colour rose. He mumbled something back, looking horrified.

The dancing stopped and everyone drifted around, forming groups and talking as they drank: Lisa and Jon joined Evan's noisy party and Evan looked at Lisa with fascinated admiration.

'You've been hiding your light under a bushel,' he told her. 'The next dance is mine.'

She was safe with Evan. He might look, but he wouldn't be tempted to touch. Anna had a chain round his neck and Evan would never stray.

Jon somehow managed to make himself scarce and Evan introduced her to some of the men in his group. They cut her out like a stray sheep and hemmed her in, talking, complimenting, flirting with her, while Evan grinned with complacent amusement behind her. She danced with one or two of them, her reckless mood making her sparkle. She caught sight of Steve now and then, dancing with other women, and when their eyes met she smiled at him, the mocking flick of her lashes covering her green eyes before he could read them.

One of her partners was an American. His brow creased as he stared down at her, the sinuous temptation of her body moving against him. 'Haven't I seen you somewhere before? I'm sure I know that face.'

'That line went out with the Charleston,' she told him, laughing.

He still stared at her in that puzzled way and later he repeated the remark when they were back with the others.

'Original, aren't you?' Evan demanded, wearing a broad grin. 'As if anyone would notice her face!'

The American shook his head. 'I'd swear I knew it. I never forget a face.'

Lisa was dancing with Evan when Steve tapped him on the shoulder. 'Mind if I cut in?'

Evan willingly moved back. 'Be my guest.' He had brought Lisa here to please Steve and his glance at her reminded her to be very nice to him. She looked away without comment, but let Steve pull her into his arms.

'What are you up to?' The harsh mutter only just reached her ears. 'I ought to slap you for this. How far do you think I'll let you go before I lose my temper?' I think you've forgotten one or two things I'll take great pleasure in bringing back to your memory.'

She raised her eyes to his face, melting in languid mockery. 'Oh? What would those be?'

'Stop flirting with every man in the room or I'll show you,' he promised.

Her hands slid along his back and she smiled slowly at him, glimmering invitation in her eyes.

His face changed. 'My God, you're asking for it!' he whispered, and his hand tightened on her waist, pulling her closer.

'Am I going to get it?'

He eyed her closely. 'Are you drunk?'

'If not I soon will be,' she decided with tongue-in-cheek gravity.

'Wait until I get you on your own,' Steve said softly.

'I'm not that reckless.' She let her cheek rest against his and felt his bones tighten as her face touched them. Her body was pulsing. She had been waiting for this all evening. They were dancing as if they were making love, the supple movements of their bodies simulating a languid passion, brushing against each other, swaying together and apart, her thigh sliding against his, the slit skirt rustling back and the sensuous line of her body pressed on him.

'If you're trying to drive me crazy you're succeeding,' he said into her ear, his lips playing with the white lobe. 'Stay off the drink, you little fool.'

The mocking green eyes gazed at him. 'I'm enjoying myself.'

'I can see that.' He spoke through barely parted lips, but the blue eyes were molten.

The beat of the music had invaded Lisa's blood. She stared at the hard bones of his face, the strong line of his mouth, then looked up into his watchful eyes.

'You're not responsible for me,' she told him, laughing. 'I'm free, I belong to myself.' She enjoyed the suppressed fury in his face. 'And there isn't a thing you can do about it,' she challenged.

'Isn't there?' The words were level. Steve didn't have the same amount of induced courage moving through his veins. He was holding his temper and his voice down.

'Nope.' She assumed a slow Western drawl. 'I'm as free as a bird, mister.'

'And what are you going to do with all this freedom?' he asked in soft, dangerous tones, his eyes glinting.

She shrugged. 'Enjoy myself. Why should I waste my life trying to convince a pigheaded, cynical swine like you that I didn't do a thing to feel guilty about except to be sorry for a man who'd spent years building up my career?'

'It all depends how sorry you were for him,' Steve bit out.

'You must have a high opinion of me if you think I'd go to bed with someone out of pity!'

She was flushed and feverish now, her voice rising.

'Be quiet,' Steve hissed. 'Do you want to tell the whole room?'

'Oh, what's the point?' she muttered wearily. 'I must be crazy. I might as well go and bang my head on a wall. You'll never believe me, will you?'

They circled in silence for a moment. 'I might believe you,' said Steve in level tones, 'but I can't get over those damned letters. You got them and you never said a word to me. Even if he never had you, letting him say such things to you was pretty close to adultery, Lisa.'

The music stopped and they drew apart. Lisa walked back to Evan and Steve vanished. Evan grinned at her. 'Getting on better with Crawford, I see.'

She shrugged. 'You said be nice to him.'

'Oh, is that what was going on?' Evan had that cynical glint in his yellow eyes. 'The way you were dancing I thought the next stop was the bedroom.'

She glared at him. Magda materialised beside them and gave Lisa a hard stare. 'Where's Steve Crawford?' she asked.

Evan chuckled, and Lisa gave him another furious look. 'How should I know?'

Magda drew her aside and lowered her voice. 'Look, Lisa, I think I ought to warn you ...'

Lisa laughed. That was hilarious. 'Warn me about Steve Crawford?' Magda was a little late with that warning. Somebody should have warned her years ago. It was too late now.

'I'm serious,' said Magda. 'I've been talking to one of his American friends.'

Lisa stiffened. 'Oh?'

'Lisa,' Magda whispered, looking around warily, 'he's married!'

Lisa laughed again. 'Did you really think he wouldn't be? A man like him?'

'Did you guess?' Magda stared at her.

'You shouldn't be so trusting,' said Lisa with barbed amusement. 'Of course someone like him was bound to be married.'

Magda looked vaguely shocked. 'You don't mind? When I saw you dancing with him I thought I ought to warn you.' She was clearly becoming disapproving. 'Do you think you should get involved with a married man?'

Lisa turned away, shrugging. She did not want to

discuss it with Magda. She had suddenly had enough of the party; she wanted to go home. Glancing around, she caught sight of Jon who backed with harassed eyes. He had kept out of her way during the last hour, and she couldn't blame him. She had been doing it deliberately. Jon had to be shown how wrong she was for him—Anna would have been dropping her elephantine hints all over the place for months and Jon was weakly susceptible to his sister's influence. Nothing Anna could say to him would persuade him to look her way again.

Drifting up to him, she announced, 'I've got a headache, Jon. Will you take me home?'

He looked relieved. 'Of course, glad to.'

Glad to get rid of her, she thought, amused. She followed him towards the door, but Steve had caught sight of their departing figures and was suddenly next to her, his hand catching her arm.

'Where are you going?' he demanded.

'I've got a headache.' It was true. Her forehead was throbbing with a sick ache right over her left eye. She recognised the symptoms. She had always been prone to migraine when she was under stress.

'Then you'd better lie down,' Steve said drily.

Jon looked at him and then just melted away like a wraith. Lisa peered after him with myopic disgust. 'Coward!' she muttered.

Steve took her waist in one arm, pulling her towards the door. 'What you need is a dark room and some peace and quiet.'

'No,' she said stubbornly, halting like a recalcitrant child.

'I can stand a scene. Can you?' He lifted a mocking eyebrow, his eyes amused.

Lisa couldn't. She could feel people staring, listening curiously to their muttered voices, not quite hearing what they were saying but trying to catch some of it.

'Damn you!' she muttered.

Steve led her out of the party and down the corridor to a room removed from the noise and confusion of the party. She turned as she saw the bed, her fingers wound through the silver fringe of her shawl.

'Don't touch me!'

Steve gave her a cool, hard little smile. 'I wasn't planning to—although you deserve a good slap. Lie down and sleep off that headache.' He switched off the light and she gave a stifled cry of panic. 'Don't be a little fool,' Steve murmured at the door, a dry thread of mockery in his voice. The door opened. The darkness was shafted with yellow light, then the door closed and she was alone.

She had sometimes had migraines during their marriage, and Steve had learnt to leave her alone in a dark, quiet room until the pain was over. She hadn't told him what was wrong, but he had probably guessed. When she began a migraine her eyes always betrayed it. Light crucified her. She had to shut her eyes to keep it out, and no doubt just now she had been peering at him like a mole.

Shakily she unzipped the dress. It slithered to the floor and she stepped out of it. When she bent to pick it up her head banged viciously and she flung the dress over a chair and groped her way to the bed to collapse on it. The ache behind her eyes was becoming nightmarish. She put her palms over her eyes and pressed them down. The darkness was shot with vivid, garish lightning that was agony. The noise of the party was muted in this room, but she could still hear it. She tried to shut it out because she had to sleep to escape this pain.

Before it reached an intolerable level she passed into sleep, her hand across her eyes in a pathetic gesture of defence. At first the sleep was light and uneasy, troubled by bad dreams, but slowly she fell into a deeper, more restful sleep, her body relaxing.

During the night she turned over heavily in sleep and collided with something warm and solid. Eyes still shut, she groped over it with one hand and heard soft laughter. She moved her head back, opened her eyes and gazed through darkness at the gleaming blue eyes staring down at her. 'Oh,' she groaned, 'you!'

'Who did you think it was?' His voice held dry sarcasm. 'Who do you usually find in your bed at night?'

'My teddy bear,' she muttered, trying to pull away but finding his muscled arm rock-hard against her back. Her fingertips had already informed her that Steve wasn't wearing a thing and her brain was working overtime assessing her situation.

'Let me go,' she told him.

'Go back to sleep, honey.' He dragged her against his chest again and his head came down on her hair. 'I'm dead,' he yawned. 'Be a good girl and shut up.'

For some reason that annoyed her. Piqued, she snuggled her cheek against him, feeling the roughness of the short dark hair rubbing her skin. Her arm slid over him and curved round his body, and she heard his heart pick up and race. His hand stroked her back and she melted against him, her lips brushing his skin, tasting the faint saltiness it left on her tongue.

'You're asking for trouble,' Steve whispered unsteadily. Is that what you want?'

Satisfied that she had aroused him, she yawned ostentatiously. 'I just want to go back to sleep,' she said, her mouth curling.

Steve said something under his breath which she decided to ignore. She lay still, aware of a warmth and security she had lacked for a long time, her ear pressed over the steady thunder of his heart, the bodily contact luxuriously comforting.

Steve must have been tired. As she herself fell back into sleep she knew from his regular breathing that he was already heavily asleep beside her, his long body relaxed but his arm still round her.

She woke up to feel lips sliding over her shoulders, tickling the faint golden hairs which from a distance did not show against the gold of her skin. She pretended to be asleep, her eyes tight shut, but the sleek movement of his limbs against her made her heart quicken. His hands moved sensuously down the curve of her spine, pressing her closer, his mouth at her throat now. Her whole body had turned boneless. She knew he must hear the shuddering breathing which betrayed she was awake and conscious of what he was doing.

She did not want to admit she was awake. She did

not want to have to decide whether to submit or not. She wanted him to take her but not present her with the responsibility for what happened.

Steve knew all that. He tipped her head back and let his mouth brush across her closed eyelids. 'You're awake, honey,' he said huskily.

Reluctantly she opened her eyes. He arched over her, his hands on either side of her head.

'Don't,' she said lamely.

Steve grinned. 'Little hypocrite!'

His mouth hungrily opened hers and she groaned as her arms went tightly round him. She knew perfectly well she wanted this to happen. She had wanted it from the moment she saw him again in that restaurant. She had been aching to be back in his arms, have him kiss her again, feel those powerful hands of his caressing her.

After the crash, Steve had made love to her with a bitter mixture of contempt and desire. Now it was different. She did not need to hear him admit how he felt: his body was shouting it at her. Steve was urgent with passion, his hands tender, his mouth demanding without cruelty.

'You're still the sexiest woman I've ever known,' he muttered huskily. 'One look at you and my hormones go crazy.'

Lisa stiffened. She was aching to have him admit he loved her, and all he could talk about was hormones: 'Let me go!' she spat furiously, shoving at his broad shoulders.

He raised his head, surprise in his face. 'What's wrong now?'

'I hate you,' she told him. 'I don't want you—let me go!'

His face was disturbingly intent, the blue eyes narrowed on her in searching enquiry. 'Like hell you don't,' he threw out. 'Just now ...'

'I was half asleep,' she lied. 'What I want is a divorce.'

'You're not getting a divorce,' Steve promised savagely. 'But you are getting me.'

'No!' She gasped as the dark head came down in bitter, searching hunger. The last of her cry was stifled as his mouth caught hers and plumbed the moist inner warmth deeply, forcing back her head with the violence of the kiss, while his hands fondled her with familiar intimacy.

She tried to move away and was caught at once by the strong hands, held prisoner. 'Stay where I want you,' he commanded.

'That's all you've ever wanted from me,' she burst out raggedly. 'I was just a thing you'd bought and could do what you liked with, wasn't I? You didn't care a damn what it did to me.'

'Are we talking about Florida?' he asked, the amusement leaving his face.

'You used me, you treated me like an animal!'

'Do you think I enjoyed it?' His eyes glittered like pieces of ice in his hard face.

'Oh, yes, I think you did! You laughed. Do you think I've forgotten that? You laughed while you humiliated me. You knew I was miserable. You knew I was sick and angry, but you deliberately set out to destroy my self-respect.'

'I wasn't feeling any too blithe myself. After nearly two years of what I'd imagined had been a perfect marriage, I discovered you'd been cheating on me with that creep Harrison.'

'I didn't, I didn't, I didn't!' she almost screamed, her face white and her mouth shaking.

Steve stared at her. She turned over and began to cry into the pillow, shuddering with sobs. His hand came down on her shoulder and stroked her gently, but she shrugged it away.

'Don't touch me! I hate the sight of you.' Her words were barely decipherable through the sobs shaking her.

He slid out of the bed and moved away. She cried until there were no tears left and then she lay there wondering what on earth she was going to do. Steve hadn't changed. If she went back to him, it would be there between them all their lives. Every time they had a quarrel it would come up again like a gas bubble through troubled water. If she looked at another man he would think of Denny and if Steve looked at another woman he would expect her to grin and bear it because of what he believed she had done.

There was no point to any of it.

She heard the chink of cups and he sank down on to the bed beside her, touching her back lightly. 'Tea,' he said quietly.

Lisa rubbed her wet face and turned reluctantly, aware that her tear-stained condition was obvious. With an averted face she sipped the tea.

'We've got to talk,' Steve told her after a moment of silence.

'I want a divorce,' she said without looking at him.

'You're not getting one.' He spoke in a crisp, determined way which left no room for argument. 'Never. I want you back. You're mine—I told you that. I never let go of what's mine.'

'Do you really think I'm weak-minded enough to come back to you and live like that for the rest of my life? I've had enough. You'll never believe me, and I'm not paying for ever for something I didn't do.'

He put down his cup. 'You won't have to,' he said harshly. 'I'm ready to believe you, Lisa.'

Slowly she raised her head, the tangled copper-coloured curls falling away from her flushed, wet face. Steve met her probing eyes directly.

'You must see how circumstantial evidence made it look,' he said in a flat voice. 'The fact that you were on your way to that cottage, the letters, the evidence my detective dug up—it all seemed pretty conclusive.'

Huskily she asked: 'And now you believe me?'

He nodded.

'Why?'

'I've had plenty of time to think in the past year. I read those letters over and over again and the dates made it obvious that if you'd had an affair with him it must have started just before the crash. He was still pleading and whining two weeks before that. I hadn't noticed the dating at the time.'

Her eyes bitter, she asked coldly: 'So you're
ready to believe circumstantial evidence but not my
word of honour?'

He moved restlessly. 'Hell, Lisa, I was out of my
mind with jealousy! All I could think of at the time
was these pictures I had in my head of the two of
you. Even after I'd noticed the way the dates didn't
fit my idea of a long affair, I still thought you'd
been going away with him that weekend. I thought
you must have finally given in to his begging.' He
hardened the line of his mouth, his eyes cold. 'But
if you say you didn't even know his plan, I'll believe
you.'

'Why?' she asked again, watching him.

He looked away, the clear sharp profile taut. Then
he said fiercely, 'Because I've got to, damn you!'

She stared at him, trying to read the averted planes
of his face. Was he trying to trap her? Was he lying
now so that she would give in and come back to him
only to revert to the torturing humiliations which
had driven her away in the first place?

Huskily, she asked: 'Why have you got to?'

He got up off the bed, his hands driven down into
the pockets of the short white robe which left bare
his hair-roughened legs, the muscular calves moving
gracefully. Walking to the window, he flicked the
cord and the blind rolled up to expose the pale morning sky which lowered with the threat of rain.

'You know damned well why,' he said. 'Since you
left me I've been going crazy. I'm an addict deprived
of his fix.' He was speaking so coolly, so levelly, that

she did not know how much of what he said to believe. 'I'm prepared to believe anything you tell me if it means I get you back in my bed.'

CHAPTER SEVEN

SHE was torn between a flicker of burning excitement at the deep note of aroused passion in his last words and a sense of anger that that was all he wanted of her. 'You mean you'll pay lip service to a pretence that I'm telling the truth, while secretly you still think Denny was my lover!'

'No,' he broke out fiercely, 'I mean what I said. I believe you, so far as it goes.'

'What does that mean?'

He swung and they stared at each other across the room with the pale light washing his skin to a faint greyness. 'I've had a lot of time to think about you in the past year,' Steve murmured. 'You're not only a very beautiful and sexy girl but you're strong, a girl with a clearly defined character. I've often found in the past that lovely girls have small brains. All their personality seems to have gone into forming the projection of themselves which they want the rest of the world to see. When I first met you, you were projecting a certain image, like it or not. Harrison managed to give you a highly sexy gloss.'

'We worked at it,' Lisa snapped. 'It was the image Denny wanted.'

He inclined his head. 'And it went like a dream, didn't it? Oh, I wouldn't dispute that Harrison was clever—in his way he was a genius. But that image of you was no more real than the costume jewellery you sometimes wore. Harrison built it up.'

She could not deny that. 'What are you getting at?' she asked him wearily. 'Where is all this leading?'

'Under the image you have brains, common sense, sensitivity,' Steve told her with clipped control. 'I was bowled over by the combination. The first time we met I just thought: Wow, I want her, and then as I got to know you I fell in love with you, the you under the Harrison mask. But although you seemed to care for me too, I slowly realised that you kept a lot of yourself back.'

'Don't we all?' Lisa rubbed her eyes with the backs of her hands, feeling the heat which smouldered deep inside the eye-sockets, the burning fever of pain and exhaustion.

'You more than most,' Steve bit out. 'I went through mask after mask, it seemed to me. You aren't a simple personality, Lisa—you're layered like a bloody cake. Whenever I reach a new dimension of you I think I've got there, only to find you've managed to fool me again.'

She raised her head in an angry motion, her eyes flashing. 'You have no right to probe into me like that! Nobody has the right to do that to another human being. We all need privacy, even if it's only the privacy of the inside of our own heads.'

Steve's blue eyes were fixed on her intently. 'There's no privacy in love, Lisa. Isn't that what it means? You've never abandoned yourself to it. You've always kept part of yourself back.'

'Always?' she asked bitterly.

He did not need to ask what she meant. His face reflected her own bitterness, his smile sarcastic. 'Oh, yes, even in Florida that week. You responded, all right, but always with that part of you standing aside. I felt like smashing your skull open to find the hidden part of you.'

She winced, horrified. She had always known that Steve was a possessive man, though he hid it well. He laughed when other men looked at her, he made light fun of the interest she aroused. But occasionally she had seen his blue eyes blaze with rage or his mouth tighten to a hard line, when someone looked at her too openly with admiration.

'That's why you go for weaklings like Harrison or Lister, isn't it?' he asked harshly. 'They're no problem. You know damned well you can run rings round them. They don't threaten that inner sanctum of yours.'

'Don't talk nonsense,' she said sharply.

'Is it nonsense?' He smiled drily. 'You know what I'm talking about, don't you? You just don't want to face up to it.'

'I don't have a clue what you mean,' she denied furiously.

'No? Doesn't it seem an odd coincidence that you picked up another clinging vine over here? Shall I tell you why, Lisa? Because it satisfies something in your nature to have that feeling of superiority over a male. You know you're stronger than Lister, just as you always knew you were stronger than Harrison. And you like that, it makes you feel good.'

'No!' Her face was washed by hot colour. 'That's a rotten accusation to make! What on earth do you think I am?'

'I wish to God I knew. Why did you let Harrison write those letters to you?'

She looked away. 'I begged him not to!'

Steve laughed curtly. 'You begged! You could have stopped them, Lisa. All you had to do was tell him you would speak to me, and they'd have stopped.'

Lisa didn't answer, but looked away.

'Shall I tell you why you didn't do that?' He sat beside her on the bed and leaned towards her, his face taut. 'Because you were enjoying it. Of course you didn't mean to go to bed with him— I've realised that. But you got a kick out of having him on his knees like that.'

'No,' she said in a muffled, shaking voice.

He caught her face in one hand, crushing her cheekbones, his thumb digging into her flesh. 'Yes,' he insisted. 'That's why you were so furious with me after Florida, why you ran— because I made you give in to me and your pride couldn't take that. That's not the way you want it, is it, Lisa? It isn't meant to be you doing the giving. It had to be the other way round. I was supposed to be on my knees, like Harrison, like Lister. That's where you want men, isn't it, Lisa? You enjoy having power over them, knowing that you're the one with the whip hand.'

Lisa tried to pull her head out of the vice in which

he held it and his hard fingers tightened, bringing
a faint gasp of pain out of her. 'Let me go!' she
wrenched out, her green eyes fire-bright.

'I went to see your mother after you'd vanished,'
Steve went on, ignoring her.

'My mother?' She sat with her eyes on his face.

'I naturally assumed you'd be in touch with her
some time, but she had no more idea where you were
than I did.' Steve surveyed her. 'You don't care
very much for your mother, do you? We saw very
little of her after our marriage.'

'She and I never got on,' Lisa said stiffly.

'You resented her remarriage, didn't you?' he
probed.

'It was her business.' Her offhand tone and shrug
did not alter Steve's watchful stare.

'I asked her about your father. From what she
said about him I got the impression of someone like
Lister; a failure, a man who never did much or got
anywhere.'

Her head lifted sharply. 'She said that?' Her voice
was filled with icy rage. 'She's lying! My father was
a gentle, sensitive man, and if he didn't achieve the
worldly success she wanted him to get, it was
largely because he wasn't cut out for the sort of job
she forced him to take. He was a teacher when they
met. Did she tell you that? And he loved teaching,
he was good at it. But that wasn't good enough for
her. She made him switch to industry. He worked in
a chemical laboratory—he was a scientist—but he
never had the drive for that sort of work. What he
wanted to do was teach. Of course he failed.'

'It was your mother who talked you into accepting a modelling career, wasn't it?'

'She admires success,' Lisa said coldy. 'Yes, she wanted me to take Denny's offer.'

'But you admire failure?' Steve smiled without humour. 'Is that what you tell yourself, Lisa?'

'Denny was not a failure! He was very successful.'

'As a photographer,' Steve agreed. 'But as a man he was negligible, wasn't he? Those letters make that obvious. You found it very exciting to watch him on his knees to you. Denny Harrison was easy to handle, wasn't he?' He tilted her head, stared into her eyes. 'I wasn't so easy, though. You wanted me too much to walk away from me and while we were married we spent so much time apart that we never had a real battle to decide who was strongest. We spent most of our marriage making love, didn't we, Lisa, and at that time we were equal. It was only when the real test came and I made you give in that you really started resenting me.'

Her face ran with angry colour, the wash of red sweeping up into her hairline. 'You didn't make me give in, Steve. You tried to destroy me. You called me a string of vile names and then forced me to behave as though I was the creature you'd called me.'

'I'd misunderstood the situation,' Steve said flatly. 'But my instinct wasn't that far wrong. You may not have committed adultery, Lisa, but we certainly didn't have a marriage of true minds. I didn't know a thing about you.'

'You still don't, if you really believe I'm the sort of woman you've just described!'

'Not consciously, perhaps,' Steve agreed levelly. 'Maybe you aren't even aware of the reasons why you let men like Lister cling round you. You're a very capable, very intelligent girl, Lisa, and you know it. You can do almost anything if you set your mind to it. But apart from me, you've either had men like Lister or you've driven off anyone who came anywhere near being your intellectual equal.'

'What you mean is that I didn't have the heart to be as ruthless with people as you always are,' Lisa accused in a low voice. 'You've always been totally ruthless with people, Steve. I've seen you in operation, remember. You use people and discard them without a scruple.'

He smiled humourlessly. 'We both do that, Lisa, only you aren't apparently even aware you're doing it. The strong always have an advantage over the weak, but the weak can twist it to their own purposes, you know. Lister is weaker than Wright, but Wright can't do a damn thing about him because Lister has him in a corner. Strength isn't always an advantage —ask Wright, if you don't believe me. He'd give his eye teeth to get rid of Lister. Lister is scared stiff of him. Yet Lister is still there.'

'Do you really think I wanted to get involved with Jon and Anna?' demanded Lisa. 'I meant to leave the agency, but Anna begged me to stay and help Jon. She's under stress already. How could I refuse?'

'I don't say you could refuse,' Steve accepted. 'But isn't it a strange coincidence that once again you're apparently being forced to connive at a situation you claim you don't want? It's a pattern, Lisa, whether you accept it or not. When you were a child I guess you watched your parents—we all do. We learn our first lessons about human nature from seeing our parents and watching them handle their relationship. What did you see, Lisa? A strong, clever woman with a drive to success having to push a weak husband into trying and failing? Did you despise your father, Lisa?'

'No, I loved him,' she burst out, so angry she almost hit him. 'I couldn't stand my mother, but I loved him.'

Steve lifted his wide shoulders in a dry shrug. 'Maybe you did, but you repeat the pattern, don't you?'

She stared at him with heated green eyes. 'I married you, not Denny! Would you call yourself a weak man, Steve?'

His smile was derisory. 'Isn't that the point? I'm not weak enough, am I, Lisa? You could never get me on my knees and you ached to get me there. I wonder if that's why you didn't choke Harrison off— did you subconsciously wonder what effect it would have on me if I feared I'd lose you? Was Harrison a club to beat me to my knees?'

'No,' she said in a high shaking voice. 'Don't be ridiculous!'

'No? That image of you that Harrison projected had that effect, though, didn't it? Most of them stared in awed adoration and kept their hands to themselves because you can freeze most men with one look. Those who wouldn't be frozen off got their faces slapped. You enjoy having that power, Lisa. It's an

inherited characteristic, maybe, and maybe you refuse to recognise it, but it's there. When you turned
on at the party tonight Lister almost ran like a rabbit. You know you can do that, don't you? You're
perfectly aware of the electric charge you carry inside yourself. You have to be, Lisa, or you couldn't
switch it off and on at will.'

Her green eyes slid away from him, uncertainty
and confusion in them. She couldn't deny some of
what he said. She had never even thought about her
parents in connection with herself, though. It was
true that she had always resented the way her mother
treated her gentle, retiring father. They had never
been suited. Lisa had been deeply attached to the
man who always seemed to have time for her when
her mother was busily engaged with other things.
After his death, her mother's rapid remarriage had
left Lisa with a burning, bitter resentment which had
still not faded.

Steve took her shoulders and turned her slowly
back towards him. 'We should have got to know each
other better. We were too busy making love to
realise that marriage can't survive just on sexual enjoyment, Lisa. It may be the most necessary ingredi-
ent of a relationship, but there's a lot more than that
to marriage. If you and I had got to know each other
better, Harrison would never have been any sort of
threat to us, would he.'

'He wasn't a threat,' she denied unsteadily. 'I've
told you . . .'

'We won't argue about it again,' Steve cut in

harshly. 'All I want is a promise from you. Will you come back with me?'

She stared at him. 'The way you've just described me I can't see how you can want me.' Her smile was sarcastic. 'You make me sound like Medusa!'

He smiled faintly. 'No, just mixed-up. We're going to unmix you.'

'What makes you think things will be any better this time?'

'I didn't know the problems before. This time I do.'

'You've left one factor out of your assessment of the situation,' Lisa said calmly.

'Oh?'

'You,' she said.

'Me?' He sounded taken aback.

She kept her eyes on his face. 'What you're offering me is a tug-of-war from which you intend to emerge the victor, Steve. You know that, don't you? You say I'm in need of power. What about you?'

'There doesn't have to be a tug-of-war,' he retorted. 'All that matters is that you accept that we're quite equal.'

She laughed. 'You're kidding!'

His blue eyes were cool and level. 'What does that mean?'

'You believe in a master race, Steve. And you're it. I had to learn that in Florida and it was an ugly lesson. You had never had to use all your force on me before, I'd given in to that charm of yours, but in Florida the mask got stripped off, didn't it? You were brutal, Steve, hard as nails and determined to the point of cruelty.'

'We've been into all that,' he brushed aside. 'It won't happen again.'

'Won't it?'

He held her eyes, his own stare narrowed and suddenly gleaming with an expression she recognised only too well. 'Whatever you are, Lisa, I want you,' he said huskily. 'If in your book that means I'm on my knees, I don't give a damn. Somehow we're going to have to learn to live together, because I can't live without you.'

She couldn't look away, her eyes were held helplessly. Steve's dark head lowered slowly and she closed her eyes. His mouth gently touched her lips and the flame shot through her. Steve pushed her back on to the bed and she briefly struggled. Their bodies tangled on the bed, his long hair-rough thigh imprisoning hers, his hands hungrily exploring her body beneath the silk slip. She tried to clear her head, but she was being swallowed into a familiar dark void in which the only thing that made any sense was the hard, naked flesh now imposing itself upon her.

'No!' she moaned, pushing at his chest and feeling the small dark hairs prickle her heated palms.

Their bodies fitted intimately, as though that instant of merging had been what both had been born for, and Lisa found it impossible to retain any shred of self-restraint or consciousness. She fought against the abandonment taking hold of her, her breath coming fiercely. Steve's blue eyes shot to her face as she struggled. 'You want it as much as I do,' he muttered grimly.

'No!' she gasped, but she was trembling. It had been too long since this aching pleasure filled her. She needed it. As she admitted that, her body yielded at last and Steve gave a hoarse cry of satisfaction.

He enforced his ownership with every driving movement of the hard body. He might have claimed that they would be equal, but although she could not doubt that her body was giving him intense pleasure, it was Steve who dominated, demanding submission, taking her fiercely.

She looked at him through her lowered lashes and saw his face a taut mask of unconcealed desire, red lying along the cheekbones, his eyes molten, his mouth partially open as he breathed painfully. Although she had given in, she was not caressing him in her turn, and Steve was aware of that and angry about it. He took her hands and lifted them to his neck, watching her. 'Touch me,' he ordered through his teeth.

He wanted her lost, driven crazy, as she had been in Florida. If she had merely submitted then it might not have been so humiliating, but although she had fought it, she had been totally abandoned in her response to his bitter lovemaking, almost as though his cruelty and force intensified her desire for him.

Her hands did not move. She saw a cool, calculating flicker of thought in the blue eyes. Then Steve bent his black head and she whimpered like a child under the ferocity of his mouth as it moved from her lips to her throat and then to her breasts. Her blood ran faster. Her eyes shut again and her hands at last moved.

It was the end of all coherent thought. She moved and groaned in a necessity which had its own reason, conscious only of an intense, burning pleasure.

When Steve had recovered his breath he rolled on to his side, his chest heaving, and regarded her with half-closed, lazy eyes. 'What did you say just now?'

Her face was burning. She didn't meet his eyes. 'I can't remember,' she lied, refusing to think of the things she had moaned into his throat.

'Funny,' he said softly, his mouth curling in mockery. 'I remember every word.'

Lisa tightened her lips angrily.

'Why do you resent feeling like that?' he asked in that soft voice. His hand closed over her naked breast in possession. 'You're fantastic. You drive me out of my mind.'

Even at the height of their lovemaking, Steve had not said he loved her. She could not doubt he had gone crazy, as he said, but it had been she who groaned words of love, not Steve.

Looking away, she caught sight of the clock and cried in horror. 'The time! I'm going to be very late for work.'

'You aren't going in to work,' Steve said flatly.

'Oh yes, I am,' she retorted.

He stared at her, his brows straight and black above the blue eyes. 'I want to get back home, Lisa. Don't drag this out. We both know you're coming with me, don't we?'

She looked down, her lids covering her green eyes,

a slight smile touching her mouth. 'Maybe I want you on your knees first,' she said in a tone as soft as his had been a moment ago.

There was a silence. His hand came up and took her chin, forced it upwards so that she looked into his eyes.

He smiled at her, warmth and amusement in the blue eyes. 'You don't want that, Lisa,' he told her. 'We just proved that, didn't we?'

'You proved what you wanted to prove,' she retorted. 'You didn't mean a word of all that talk of equality, Steve. We both know you have every intention of being master, in or out of bed. You only know one way of making love, showing it.'

His mouth twitched derisively. 'And you didn't enjoy it?'

Her flush deepened and she didn't answer.

'I'm not one of your clinging vines, Lisa. I have no intention of begging. You're coming back to me on my terms, but I meant it when I said they were terms of equality. If you can't see that even in bed we're equals you aren't thinking straight. Yes, I was the one doing the taking, but you were giving, Lisa, and I don't have to tell you how you made me feel. We're equal, but we aren't identical.'

Her eyes questioned him dubiously although she did not ask aloud what he meant.

He smiled again with sardonic emphasis. 'You're a woman, Lisa, not a man. In my bed I'm the one who dominates, but that doesn't make us enemies. It's perfectly natural. The act of love was designed by nature, not by man. I didn't invent it. I'm a man and that means I've a normal sex drive. But I don't want a passive, submissive victim in my bed: I want you the way you were just now. Would you call that submission, Lisa?' The blue eyes mocked her. 'Don't you know how wild you are in bed?'

She dropped her eyes, her face hot and confused. Steve laughed and kissed her hard.

'Yes,' he whispered. 'You know, all right. You didn't want to respond like that, but you did and you always have. That's why I went crazy when I imagined you with Harrison. I couldn't stand the thought of anyone else with you. But then he would never have got that sort of passion out of you, would he, my darling? Because deny it though you may, you only really turn on when I force it out of you. You may claim you want equality, but sexually you don't want anything of the kind.'

'Oh, shut up!' she muttered.

Steve laughed again. 'Hit a nail on the head, did I?'

Lisa didn't answer. Steve's hand was stroking softly down her body and raising far too many ripples of excitement and he was doing it quite deliberately. He had presented her with a problem and she did not know what she was going to do about it.

CHAPTER EIGHT

LISA walked into the agency, shaking her umbrella free of the clinging drops of rain. Outside the sky was a looming grey, clouds shedding their moisture in a steady downpour which had forced shoppers and workers to hurry along, heads bent, moving even faster than normal at this hour of the morning. The receptionist glanced up and smiled at her. 'Another beautiful day,' she remarked sarcastically.

Lisa smiled back and walked across to the lifts. When she emerged on the floor which housed Wrights, she ran almost at once into Magda, who gave a muffled exclamation.

'Where have you been all night?' She whispered it with a glance over her shoulder. 'Lisa, you weren't with him?'

Flushing, Lisa made a face. 'That isn't a question you should ask or I intend to answer,' she retorted, moving past her.

Magda watched her, disapproval in her face, and Lisa realised that she was not going to escape a post-mortem from Magda when they were alone in the flat. Raging curiosity vied with Magda's moral outrage. It was time she told the truth, Lisa realised. She did not want to have Magda going around like the ghost of Hamlet's father, pointing a spectral finger at her for ever.

141

In her own office she dropped her damp umbrella into the umbrella stand, hung up her raincoat and glanced at her reflection in the small mirror.

Her face had a distinct pallor which her careful make-up could not disguise. She had not resolved the problem which Steve had presented her with—they had discussed it for an hour before she returned home to change out of her white dress. Steve had driven her to the flat and left her, at her request, although he had wanted to wait and drive her on to the office. Lisa had been very relieved to find that Magda had already left. The last thing she had been in the mood for had been a question-and-answer session with a horrified flatmate. She had realised that Magda was bound to be absolutely palpitating with curiosity, but she had not made up her mind how to reply to her.

She was working on some letters when Jon looked round the door at her. His eyes did not quite meet hers and she knew that that was for a mixture of reasons. Jon had ducked out last night and he was not quite sure how she would feel about that, also in all probability he had put two and two together when she vanished with Steve like that without returning. He must have driven Magda home later and Lisa could imagine what the two of them supposed was happening between her and Steve.

So this morning Jon was embarrassed, his face rather sheepish and flushed. Maybe he thought that she would be angry with him because he had recoiled from her. Lisa had no intention of explaining to him that her femme fatale act had been partly designed to terrify the wits out of him.

Raising her head, she smiled. 'Hallo,' she said brightly.

Jon muttered a reply. 'You're in, then.' He cut that off with a very audible gulp because he did not want to tread on to any difficult ground. 'Good,' he said vaguely. 'Good.' He vanished again and she couldn't help laughing silently as the door closed. Poor Jon!

Evan was rather more difficult and rather more straightforward. He blew into the room like a dust-storm and halted to eye her with a ribald amusement he did nothing to hide. 'Hallo there. I thought we might not see you today.'

'I work here,' she said coolly, meeting his amused stare.

'And very adequately too,' he agreed. 'I might even raise your salary.'

She did not need to ask why, but her lips shut firmly on a furious outburst. She offered him a red herring. 'How's Anna?' she asked.

He perched on the edge of her desk like an elephant on a drum. 'I've been talking to her on the phone. She's bored but resigned. Why don't you drop in to see her?'

Lisa smiled. 'I'd love to.' She wouldn't just yet, however, because Anna would want to talk about Jon and Lisa was not going anywhere near her until Anna knew about Steve. 'How are the boys bearing up?'

'Catherine copes with them very well, but they hanker after Anna.' He grimaced. 'So do I, God knows. The house seems so damned empty without her. I hate going home when she isn't there. Catherine does her best, but it isn't the same.'

'Anna will be home soon,' Lisa reassured him. 'She's having a rest, that's the main thing.'

The door behind them both swung open and Evan glanced round, only to look drily amused as he saw Steve. He slid off Lisa's desk. 'You don't want me, I imagine?' he said with resigned emphasis.

Steve was expressionless. 'No,' he agreed. 'I want my wife.'

For a moment Evan did not react. His face was totally blank. Then he looked at Lisa, his heavy head turning slowly, and back at Steve.

'Come again?'

'My wife,' said Steve still in that calm voice, his face turned towards Evan as though he were making some normal conversational sally. 'I'm taking her out to lunch.' He looked at Lisa at last. 'Ready, Lisa?'

She didn't move, her hands folded in her lap. Evan wasn't going to let them walk out with that revelation hanging in the air. He was gaping at her dumb-founded, a question in his eyes.

'Are you telling me you two have got married?' His voice rose to a pitch near a squeak. 'My God, that was fast work!' The yellow eyes gazed at Lisa glow-ingly. On someone's part, his eyes said, and asked silently if it had been brilliant strategy on Lisa's side which had resulted in marriage.

Steve pushed his hands into his pockets, his dark head on one side. 'We've been holding back on you, I'm afraid,' he said in that quiet voice. 'Lisa and I have been married for three years.'

Evan's mouth opened but did not shut and no

words came out. Steve smiled faintly, watching his astounded face.

'We needn't go into the details, but a year ago we separated—now I'm taking Lisa back to the States with me.'

She looked down at her hands. He had no right to walk in here and make such a statement. She had given him no answer yet. She had listened to him, but she hadn't said she was prepared to try again.

Evan was rarely lost for words. He sank back into a chair and looked from one to the other of them. 'You're a couple of cool customers, I must say. Why did you keep it quiet?'

'That's our business.' Steve softened that with a polite little smile, the blue eyes not unfriendly.

Lisa could see Evan desperately searching his mind for the memory of whatever he had said about her to Steve and, probably, vice versa. He was flushing slowly as he recalled the way he had asked her to 'be nice' to Steve. What, she wondered drily, had he said on the quiet to Steve about her? Evan was not above selling her verbally to Steve as a possible conquest. He had wanted to use her as bait and now he was kicking himself. He was irritated with them, too, of course, because he was beginning to feel a fool.

'I had no idea Lisa had ever been married,' he muttered. 'She never even hinted.'

Steve shrugged. 'I realise it will make a difficulty for you if she leaves at once, but I'd like you to release her as soon as possible. The contract is yours, by the way, but not with Lister in charge.' His mouth twitched into a slight smile which had no humour in it. 'He hasn't got the capacity. I want you. I'm afraid my main idea in coming to the agency was to get Lisa back. I'm telling you frankly because you're too bright not to work that one out for yourself when you get around to thinking about it. The contract was just bait I was dangling to give myself an excuse for seeing her, but I'll honour my word, so long as you handle it yourself. Lister may be your brother-in-law, but he's a fool. If I were you, I'd find him a sinecure somewhere else.'

'Do you think I wouldn't give my eye teeth to do just that? My wife would probably leave me.'

'Can't you find him something he wants to do? If your wife imagines it's his own decision, she won't kick up a fuss.'

Evan sighed. 'What, though? Jon has no ambitions elsewhere. Who'd take him on? One look at him and any sane man is going to say clear off.'

'You aren't fair to him,' Lisa burst out. 'Jon is very methodical and careful. He would make a good clerk or an accountant. Just because his talents don't lie in the same direction as yours it doesn't mean he doesn't have talents.'

Both men looked at her as though a sheep had opened its mouth and talked. Evan patted her cheek paternally and then gave Steve a slightly nervous look, suddenly remembering she was his wife.

'You're a kind-hearted girl,' he said, moving away from her in an obvious fashion.

She met Steve's eyes, glaring at him. He despised Jon, as he had despised Denny, because his own strength and arrogance made life so simple for him.

Steve thrived on challenge. He had a hard, clear mind and an unbounded confidence in himself. Maybe that was why he had been so violently angry when he thought she had been unfaithful to him—Steve had found the blow to his confidence too great to bear. His temper had turned to bitter cruelty. But if he took that contract away from Jon now and gave it to Evan, there was going to be trouble.

'Jon ought to get another job,' she said sharply. 'And while Anna is in hospital it could all be arranged before she found out about it.'

'That's true,' said Evan, looking eager, then his face fell into defeated lines again and he sighed. 'But what? Got any bright ideas?'

Steve glanced at Lisa, his brows drawn into a dark line across his forehead, the blue eyes clear and thoughtful. 'I could find him a place,' he murmured.

Evan's yellow stare widened. 'Are you kidding?'

'I imagine we could fit him in somewhere.' Steve gave a slightly contemptuous shrug. 'My New York office can always accommodate one more idiot. He can start in the accounts department and we'll see how he does there. He could take some night school training—he isn't too old to learn a new profession.'

Evan seized Steve's hand and wrung it. 'My God, you don't know what you'd be doing for my marriage!'

'I've an idea,' Steve commented drily. 'Lisa gave me some hints about the set-up.'

'Jon hasn't agreed yet,' Lisa pointed out a little tartly.

Evan's teeth bared. 'He will,' he promised. 'My

God, he will. When can he start?'

He wanted to get it all wrapped up and turned into a fait accompli before Anna heard about it, of course. If Evan had his way, Jon would be out of the country and safely in the States before his wife got wind of these plans.

Steve laughed flatly. 'I'll arrange it at once. He can fly over at the end of the month, find somewhere to live and sort out all the details.'

Evan rubbed his hands, beaming with delight. 'I really appreciate this, Steve.'

'Good,' Steve drawled. 'Then you can release my wife at the end of this week, I hope?'

'Of course,' Evan agreed, nodding his large head. He gave Lisa one of his sly glances, his eyes amused. 'You live in California, I take it?'

'Right on the other side of the country from New York,' Steve said with unhidden satisfaction. 'I don't wish your brother-in-law any harm, but the less I see of him the better.'

Evan grinned. 'I get the same feeling. Every time I see him my foot itches.'

They exchanged conspiratorial laughter and Lisa fumed. Such big strong men! she thought, glaring at them. They both had that dynamic energy, the forceful hard-eyed certainty of men who know where they are going and have no time for those who lack their own drive.

Steve glanced at his watch. 'I've booked a table,' he said to her. 'Are you coming?'

She gathered her things together and stood up. Evan winked at her. 'You might have given me a hint,' he told her. 'I could have put my foot right in it.'

'What do you mean, could have?' she asked pointedly, walking to the door, and knowing she had had a slight revenge because Evan had looked appalled at once, his eyes flying to Steve as though afraid of his reaction. Now Evan would sit and search his mind for anything he might have said to her about Steve. Serves him right! she thought.

Over lunch Steve gave her a considering, ironic smile. 'Annoyed with me?'

'What on earth makes you think that?' she asked with sarcasm, her green eyes cold.

He grinned, undeterred. 'I thought so. You've hardly said a word since we left the agency. All I've got out of you have been a few icy syllables.'

'What do you expect? You had no business walking in and dropping that bombshell without consulting me first.'

Steve shrugged his broad shoulders, the black head tilted in cool contemplation of her face. 'I decided it was time to cut the knot. You would have drifted on for weeks before you came to a decision.'

'Isn't that my privilege?'

'No,' he pronounced decisively. 'I haven't got time to wait for you to make up your mind.'

'What if I say I'm not coming back with you?'

'You will,' he said with a trace of insolence.

Lisa's colour washed up to her hairline, the gleam of her golden skin lost in a deep flush. 'You're too damned sure, then.'

He leaned across the table and took her hand, although she tried to pull it away. Raising it to his lips he kissed the palm, his mouth cool on her skin. The wicked blue eyes teased her. 'I'm not the only one who's addicted, am I, Lisa?'

No, she thought, meeting that bright stare. She could hardly deny that to him after the way she had responded to him earlier that day. But then Steve had always known he could get her. When he saw her again in that restaurant his eyes had been as arrogantly confident as ever. He had never doubted that sooner or later he would get her back. She felt the moist touch of his tongue in the centre of her palm and shivered, her eyes falling. He laughed softly.

'You're not pushing me around,' she announced, dragging her hand out of his grasp.

He refused to hurry the pace at which he ate the meal, deliberately lingering over it, enjoying the irritation with which she watched him. She could hardly just walk out. She was forced to sit there and watch him with a deep desire to hit him with something.

'You're not going back to the agency,' he told her, when they did leave the restaurant halfway through the afternoon.

'I can't just walk out on them!'

'You can and you will,' Steve informed her. He drove her back to her flat, however, and said he was not coming in with her. 'I've got our arrangements to make. I'll fix our flight and let you know tomorrow.'

She was surprised that he was leaving her alone and he saw that from the way she glanced obliquely at him, smiling at her.

'You need time to think,' he murmured. 'We both do. We're both of us strong characters, honey. Maybe our marriage is bound to be a fight, but it will have its compensations. Fights that end in bed have their own singular excitement, remember.'

'You can't just wipe out the past, though,' she protested. 'I don't know that I want to live with a man who could behave the way you did in Florida.'

'Do you think I didn't ask myself if I wanted to live with a woman who could let Harrison write those letters to her?' he demanded.

He ran his hand under her hair, his fingers teasing her warm nape. 'I was forced to realise then that it wasn't a question of whether I could live with you but whether I could live without you. Ask yourself that, honey, and answer it honestly.' His mouth came down and crushed her lips, burning against them, opening them and draining her of the response he wanted. When he drew back she was breathing thickly, her green eyes smouldering behind her lowered lids. Steve opened the car door for her and she climbed out unsteadily. He shot away, leaving her staring after him.

Lisa sat in the flat with fixed green eyes like a sphinx staring at nothing. Could she bear to contemplate life without him? She had spent the last year in a limbo of loneliness and aching need. Was that how she was prepared to spend the rest of her life? The chance of ever meeting anyone who could affect her the way Steve did was highly remote. In the years before she met him there had never been anyone else, and she doubted if there ever would be again.

He had infuriated her with his view of her. She was not some sort of power-mad female determined to force the opposite sex to its knees. Steve had twisted the peculiar circumstances in which she had been trapped. Jon was not another Denny; he was just a rather helpless man without any ability to break free of his situation. Lisa didn't even want Jon to care for her; she never had. Steve had been theorising about her and he had got his theory twisted because the premise had been false. She had learnt by observing her parents, it was true, but what she had learnt had been that it was impossible for her to hurt a weaker human being. Her mother had bullied her father, but Lisa had never been tempted to bully either Denny or Jon. On the contrary, she had been trapped by them because of her dislike of hurting people. That was what she had been taught by her parents.

Of course, it was true that she avoided relationships with men on the whole, but largely because so few of them could be trusted to keep their hands to themselves. Steve had never been a woman in the fashion world. He wouldn't realise the problems women came up against. Too many men saw women in purely physical terms.

Even Steve, she thought angrily. He hadn't breathed a word of love to her. He had talked of needing her, wanting her, desiring her. But he hadn't said he loved her.

What did Steve know of her? And what did she know of him? They had been married for two years, but during those years both of them had been absorbed in their own careers and their meetings were all on a purely physical level. She had learnt that Steve was clever, tough, devious; a man with enough brains to know what he wanted and enough arrogance to go after it without caring for the consequences for anyone else. She knew he liked hard plain chocolates, although he ate them very rarely. She knew he liked sunbathing as much as she did, that he swam like a fish and liked to surf on the Florida beaches. She knew he loved jazz, particularly traditional jazz; that he read fast modern thrillers and liked driving fast cars. His favourite colours, his taste in foods, his ability to take brief naps during the day so that he could work until late into the night, his fury when he had even a mild illness; she knew all these. They were the small details which one picked up from living with someone, but they did not explain the man underneath.

We all theorise about each other, try to fit the small clues we see into a firm pattern which can explain the personality, but there is often a hidden key we do not find, a clue we are not shown, and that can be decisive.

Steve did not understand her and she did not understand Steve. Would it be madness to try to reform their marriage? When they had run into trouble, they had savaged each other and split apart. Would it happen again?

But then she faced his last question and covered her face with her trembling hands. Could she live without him?

Steve was right, she realised. He might be a dark maze into which she had wandered blind and through which she had no thread to guide her, but when she considered life without him it looked far darker and more lonely.

When he made love to her he wrung out of her an anguished passion which made life bearable for those few moments. In abandoning herself in his arms she reached some sort of equilibrium which the rest of life never offered her. Perhaps it was the same for Steve. He had not asked her to say she loved him— she had moaned that out involuntarily and his blue eyes had had a brilliant smile in them, although he had teased her about it afterwards. Steve had not been mocking her maliciously at that moment. There had been warmth in his eyes, not malice.

Once during the first months of their marriage they had been at a Los Angeles nightclub together, dancing in the minute space, the heavy beat of jazz filling the small cellar, when Steve had tightened his arms round her and put his cheek against hers. 'Honey, I love you,' he had muttered hoarsely. 'Let's get out of here. This isn't what I want to do.'

They had gone home and made love in a hectic silence, the heat between them burning along her veins. Steve was the sort of man who has a deep sense of possession towards his woman. He demonstrated it in many ways, of course, but chiefly in their bed, and it had been the outrage to his sense of possession which had made him so cruel in Florida. Many men in his position would undoubtedly have gone on to divorce their erring wife. Steve had merely enforced his ownership over and over again. He hadn't told her again that he loved her. Had his love been smothered when he believed she was Denny's mistress? Or was he merely refusing to say it aloud?

Lisa was still sitting there when Magda burst into the flat. She halted, staring at Lisa, her eyes popping out of her flushed face.

'Is it true? Evan's pulling my leg, isn't he? It can't be true!' Her voice was breathless and ragged, and for a few seconds Lisa hoped Magda hadn't taken Steve too seriously because that would be a most unfortunate complication.

Slowly, watchfully, she nodded.

'Jumping Jehosaphat!' Magda almost shrieked. 'You are the most secretive, sneaky, lying two-faced ...' She broke off, sitting down. 'Go on, you're pulling my leg!' she said with a grin. 'It's one of Evan's big jokes. It isn't April Fool's Day, you know.'

Lisa looked at her. She was sitting cross-legged on their little sofa with her toes wreathed in a semi-lotus position, her slender back graceful. 'I'm Steve Crawford's wife,' she told Magda. 'I'm sorry I kept it a secret from you, but you see, Steve and I had separated and I didn't plan to go back to him.'

'I just knew you two were fated,' Magda sighed romantically. 'The day he walked into the office I could feel the vibrations.'

Lisa smothered a smile. She didn't remember it that way. Magda had been convinced Steve fancied her, but then Steve had deliberately given that impression. He could say what he liked about her using people, but he did it quite ruthlessly.

'And now you're going back to him?' Magda prompted. 'Evan said you were.'

'I suppose I am,' said Lisa on a sigh. Of course she was, why was she pretending even to need to think about it?

Magda gazed at her. 'How could you leave him in the first place? I'm absolutely crazy about the way he talks!'

'That,' Lisa said coolly, 'is a coldblooded and deliberate imitation of a Southern accent. Steve's a Californian born and bred and his natural accent isn't anywhere near as soft and drawling as that. He only does that sexy drawl when he's up to something.'

'As far as I'm concerned he can do it all the time,' said Magda with unhidden enthusiasm. 'And I don't need telling what he's up to—those gorgeous blue eyes make that quite clear!'

Lisa laughed reluctantly. 'So they do.' Oh, yes, she thought.

'Bedroom eyes,' Magda groaned, 'that's what he's got.'

'That's my husband you're talking about,' Lisa said with amusement.

Magda grinned at her. 'I can look, can't I?'

'No,' Lisa told her, but smiled.

Magda's face sobered. 'Jon looked as if he'd been knocked for six, by the way.'

Lisa lost her smile. 'Did he?' She paled slightly. 'Did he say anything?'

Magda shrugged. 'I just saw him walk past. He looked dazed. I said hallo and he didn't even hear me.'

Guiltily, Lisa said: 'Jon wasn't in love with me!'

'No?' Magda stared at her. 'I always wondered why you ever went out with him at all, he's such a bore. I can't stand men who haven't got any backbone.'

Lisa didn't say anything for a moment, then she said: 'Did Evan tell you Steve has offered Jon a job in New York?'

'Tell us?' Magda giggled. 'Evan was crowing all over the office about it. It was his big day. He must think it's Christmas!'

'I hope Jon was pleased about it,' Lisa said anxiously.

'Never mind Jon,' Magda clicked. 'Tell me all about Steve.' She looked hard at Lisa. 'You really have been very sly. You gave me the impression you didn't even like him and when I told you I'd heard he was married you didn't give me so much as a hint that it was you!'

Lisa told her as little as she could, skating over the details without revealing anything of the real background, leaving Magda with the deliberate impression that she and Steve had merely quarrelled and split up a year ago but were now reconciled.

'Did he come over to find you again?' Magda asked, her eyes alight with romantic eagerness.

Lisa smiled. 'What do you think?'

Magda groaned. 'You are lucky! I just don't know how you could leave him in the first place. I'd have padlocked him to my wrist if I'd been you.'

'Maybe I will in future,' Lisa said lightly.

'You'd better,' Magda told her. 'I might just try to

steal him if you leave him lying around again!'

She went off at last to bath and change and Lisa went to the phone. Evan answered it and she asked him directly: 'How did Jon take it?'

'Like a man with shellshock,' Evan said bluntly. 'I barely got a word out of him. He just stared.'

'Oh, dear!'

'I don't know which piece of news hit him hardest —your marriage or the offer of a job in New York.'

'Did he say whether he'd take the job?' asked Lisa.

'Of course he'll take it,' Evan told her.

'Did he say he would?'

'Yes.' Evan was firm on that. 'In fact, if anything he seemed relieved. He knows as well as we do that it just isn't working for me to have him under my feet all day. Sooner or later I'd have gone through the roof and then Anna might have left me.'

'I'm sure she'd do nothing of the sort,' Lisa said without real belief.

'You know damned well she would,' Evan grunted. 'I love Anna, but I'm sick of getting her brother rammed down my throat.'

'When are you going to tell Anna?'

'Jon and I are going to the hospital together to-night. I've made it clear to Jon that he's got to make Anna think it's his idea—if she believes he wants a job in the States, she'll accept it. Jon is going to sell her the idea that it's a much better job with bigger prospects and that he's sick of advertising.'

'I'm sure he is,' Lisa murmured drily.

'So am I,' said Evan, and chuckled in his deep, sardonic fashion. 'So is Anna, I've no doubt, so with just a little luck my tangled life is going to get straightened out at last. If Anna has the baby without any further troubles and Jon clears off to the States, my life is going to be all sunshine from now on.'

'Lucky you,' Lisa said sarcastically.

Evan was silent for a few seconds, then he asked quietly: 'Isn't yours, Lisa? You and Crawford—it is all right, isn't it?'

She was touched by the serious concern in his voice and smiled. 'Yes, Evan, Steve and I are going to be all right.'

When she had rung off she looked at the phone. She had told Evan that without much hesitation, but was it even partially true? She knew she was going back to Steve, but what sort of marriage were they going to have this time? For the second time in her life she was walking blind into a dark maze.

CHAPTER NINE

ANNA lay back against her pillows, the afternoon sunlight streaming in through the slatted blinds and illuminating her flushed face, giving a brightness to her fair hair. A vast spray of roses stood on the bedside locker at one side of her, their heavy perfume filling the room and drowning the astringent scents of the hospital. Over her lace-trimmed nightie she wore a delicate pink bedjacket with trailing pink satin ribbons with which she was playing absently as she stared at Lisa.

'You might have told me.' Her soft mouth had a discontented droop. 'No wonder you wouldn't even consider Jon!' She slid her eyes down to the pile of magazines which Lisa had brought her and which lay on the bed. 'I'm surprised you ever went out with him.'

'Jon and I were always just friends.' Lisa had no difficulty in catching the slight criticism implied in Anna's voice.

'But he didn't know you were married.' Anna raised her eyes. 'Don't you think that was rather unfair?'

Lisa flushed slightly. 'I suppose it was.'

Anna stared hard at her. 'You suppose? You know it was! You had no business going out with Jon when you were already married. If you'd told him it would have been different, but you didn't, did you? Jon knew no more than the rest of us.'

Lisa bit her lip. She had felt she had come to see Anna for the last time and she had expected disapproval, but it was still painful to see that coldness in Anna's eyes. She had become fond of her during the last year.

'And now your husband is taking Jon off to the States.' Anna's voice hardened. 'Guilty conscience, Lisa?'

Lisa's green eyes widened and flashed. 'Of course not! I had absolutely nothing to do with Steve offering him the job. Steve had just gathered that Jon wasn't too keen on advertising and he had an opening in New York which he thought Jon could fit.'

'I hope this job is as good as Evan claims,' Anna said tightly. 'I wouldn't want Jon getting stuck in some dead-end job in a foreign country. He wouldn't tell us if he hated it, and how are we to know when we're so far away?'

Anna was disturbed by the prospect of her brother being outside her sphere of influence. For most of his life, Jon had been close to her, protected by her, managed by her. Anna might at some level of her mind be aware that Jon was ruining her marriage, but she still found it hard to let him go. Were people always empire-builders? Always trying to establish bridgeheads in other people's lives, extending their power to cover other territory and fighting to the death to stop that power being taken away from them?

'Jon will soon find his feet,' Lisa murmured. 'Steve and I will keep an eye on him. Of course, we'll be in California, but Steve often goes to New York, and he'll take a personal interest in Jon.' She was not going to tell Anna that part of Steve's 'personal interest' would be in making sure that Jon stayed in New York and never came within a mile of Lisa.

Anna's eyes watched her sharply. 'Steve isn't jealous of Jon, then?'

Lisa looked at her and smiled. 'Of course not. Steve knows there was never anything romantic between Jon and me. I made that quite clear to you all the way, Anna—you can't say I didn't. And I made it quite clear to Jon too.'

Anna made a dissatisfied sound.

'How's the baby?' Lisa asked to change the subject.

Anna's face softened. 'Growing again,' she admitted. 'I had a sonic test yesterday. They said the growth had started again and things are going to be fine.'

'I'm glad,' Lisa told her warmly. 'Evan will be so relieved. He's been like a bear with a sore head while you were away.'

'I know!' Anna laughed, but her eyes were warm. 'Poor darling, he does so hate it when I'm away.'

'What is a sonic test?' Lisa asked.

'I'm not sure how it works. They say it's rather like the method used to discover submarines under the sea. They swing something over your tummy and it gives off sound waves or something, then they draw these on a graph and it shows the outline of the baby, so they can see how it's lying and how big it is.' Anna's laughing eyes held Lisa's. 'They did explain it to me, but I was so nervous I didn't take it all in the first time and I don't like to ask them again.'

'Isn't science marvellous?' Lisa laughed back at her.

'It is,' Anna said soberly. 'If they hadn't discovered that the baby wasn't doing well things might have been pretty hairy. I might have lost it.'

'Then Evan would have gone mad,' Lisa agreed. 'He's praying it's a girl, isn't he?'

Anna giggled. 'So he says, but I'm not so sure. Evan likes his boys.'

Lisa gave her a wicked grin. 'He rather likes girls too.'

Anna laughed.

'And he's hoping it will look like you,' Lisa told her.

Anna's smile was relaxed and happy. 'I know. Oh, under all that bluster, Evan's as soft as butter.'

'Where you're concerned,' Lisa reminded her. 'I'm not so sure about the rest of the world.'

She left Anna on a last exchanged smile and walked out of the hospital, relieved to have ended on a friendly note. Anna was not happy at the prospect of Jon going away, but once the new baby was there to occupy her mind she would get used to the idea.

After work that day there was to be a party at the agency for her. It had been Evan's idea. 'We've got a lot to celebrate,' he had told her.

'You have,' she had teased, and he had grinned unashamedly.

'You can say that again! I knew the day you walked in here that you would do us nothing but good, and I was right. You've propped Jon up for the last year and now you're whisking him out of my life at last. Anna and the baby are fine. The sun is shining and I'm on top of the world.'

She had laughed, 'Egotist!'

'That's me.' Evan didn't care if people thought him an egotist. He only really cared for Anna and at last he was going to get her all to himself. He had never been jealous of his wife's loving devotion to their children—as an extension of himself, the two boys were no threat to him. Evan would happily share Anna with their children, but he did not want anyone else walking inside the magic circle of his life with her.

When men learnt to talk in the beginning of the civilised world they used language not as a means of communication alone but as a means of excluding others—using it as a way of setting themselves apart and shutting out strangers. Marriage had something of the same reason. Lisa had often noticed that newlyweds tended to lose interest in their old friends, to change their habits, to establish new ones which were a cement for the marriage and a method of excluding others.

From the beginning of his marriage Evan had had Jon around his neck like an albatross. Now Jon was going, and Lisa hoped Evan would achieve the heavenly bliss he appeared to expect.

She and Steve were booked on a flight at ten o'clock next morning. They would not be staying too late at the party, although Evan intended it to go on for hours. Lisa had wound up her affairs in London very rapidly. Magda had already found herself a new flatmate, one of the other girls from the agency, and Evan had interviewed someone for Jon's job. It was really all settled, and Lisa wished she did not feel quite so uneasy and uncertain.

She had accepted that she couldn't live without Steve. Now the only question she had to settle was: how could she live with him?

And that was not a question with an easy answer.

She had moved into Steve's flat two days ago, but he had had a good deal of business to get through in

London and they had only seen each other in the evenings since she joined him.

When she reached the flat after visiting Anna she found Steve lounging on the long cushioned couch reading a newspaper. He tilted his black head backwards as she came into the room.

'Where have you been?' he asked.

'Visiting Anna,' she told him.

He caught her wrist as she walked past and pulled her down to kiss him. When he released her, she straightened, flushed, and the blue eyes observed her mockingly.

'Stop fighting it,' he advised, tongue-in-cheek.

'Have you?' She walked into the bedroom and unzipped her dress. Steve lounged in the doorway, watching her slender figure in the black silk slip.

'Yes,' he said quietly. 'It took a while for me to realise that I wanted a lot more from you than just the pleasure you give me in bed, but yes, I've stopped fighting it.'

She looked at his reflection in the mirror, the lean graceful lines of his body oddly distant. He might claim he had stopped fighting, but he still hadn't said he still loved her. Maybe he didn't still love her. Maybe he resented the fact that she affected him the way she did.

That was how she felt, she knew that. She wanted him, she loved him, but she was angry at her own weakness.

'Hadn't you better change? The party begins at seven, remember.' She walked into the bathroom and

closed the door, aware of him watching her every
inch of the way with an unreadable expression. She
was in flight from him even now and Steve was aware
of it. They were both far too aware of each other,
each nervously alert to every signal emanating from
the other.

Steve was ready before she was, which was no surprise, but he showed no impatience as he sat casually
reading his newspaper. Looking up as she joined him,
the blue eyes skimmed coolly over her, only the brief
flash in them revealing to her the effect she had had.

'Switched on, are we?' he asked drily, and her
colour mounted for an angry second.

She was wearing black, his favourite colour, and
the sophisticated sheath left little to the imagination,
laying bare her shoulders, arms and throat and giving
tantalising glimpses of her breasts.

Steve stood up, throwing aside his newspaper, and
she glanced aside nervously from the impact of his
long, hard body under that closely-cut suit. Her
mouth went dry and her lashes flickered. He walked
towards her and she looked back at him, the green
eyes revealing.

Steve stopped in front of her and looked down
with narrowed, gleaming eyes. 'Shall we skip the
party?' The deep husky voice made her shiver.

'Don't be absurd,' she muttered shakily.

His long fingers slid silkily along her arm. 'Don't
forget how well I know you, my darling,' he whispered.

'The party is for us, remember?' She pulled her
arm back and moved away towards the door. Steve

sauntered after her, but as they stood in the lift going
down to the underground car park there was a dark
glitter in his eyes as he watched her averted profile.
Steve had no illusions about the struggle going on inside her. They had made love several times since she
joined him at the flat, but Lisa was still eluding him
and Steve knew it. Although he was saying nothing,
he was annoyed, and beneath his mocking smile she
could see that anger even now.

Steve was demanding total capitulation on her
part while himself remaining free. She did not know
what was going on inside his head. He had said a
good deal, but how much of it did he mean? The
memory of those bitter nights with him a year ago still
haunted her. Had he worn out the torturing jealousy
in the year apart from her, or was it all still there
smouldering under his smooth surface, waiting to
break out again once he had her safely back in California?

Everyone had a series of façades, masks, pretences
which they showed the world. Lisa did not know how
much of what Steve had said about her own masks
was true—did one ever know anything about one-
self? But Steve had his own deceiving images: the
charm and good looks which he used to coax response
out of people, the shrewd toughness which ran a
wealthy and growing company, the harsh cruelty
which had forced her to her knees and mocked her
inability to resist him.

She felt like someone in a fairground seeing dis-
solving, deceptive mirrors in which shadowy figures
moved.

Which was Steve? What was he really like? What were his real intentions?

He was asking her to trust herself to him when he was not allowing her to see what he was really like.

Evan greeted them jovially when they arrived. The room was packed with members of staff who were already in a very lively mood and the amount of drink being consumed suggested that tomorrow they were none of them going to be in much of a mood for work.

Evan inspected Lisa with flushed admiration, patting her arm while his leonine eyes wandered over the rest of her. 'My God, the office will be duller without you,' he said loudly.

Steve's smile was cool. Evan gave him a brief teasing grin and Lisa saw that Evan was not above deliberately trying to get a rise out of him.

'Come and have a drink with me, my lovely,' he told her, his arm going round her waist.

She did not protest or unlink herself. Evan had no more real interest in her than in the office desks, but he had been drinking, he was on top of the world, and, in typical masculine fashion, he was preening himself like an infatuated peacock.

'I saw Anna today,' she told him.

His eyes gleamed like golden coins. 'Looking better, isn't she?'

'Much more rested,' she agreed. 'And the baby is fine now. I'm so glad about that, Evan.'

'We can have her home in a couple of weeks,' he said in satisfaction. 'I've promised to keep her in bed as much as possible. She has to have at least three hours' rest a day from now on until the baby arrives.'

Jon was on the far side of the room and had his back to her. Lisa had not seen him since he heard the news about her marriage. She glanced at him and Evan caught her brief look and smiled at her.

'Forget him,' he told her. 'He's fine. Jon hasn't got the capacity to feel much—didn't you realise that? He worries, but mostly about himself.'

She laughed reluctantly. 'You're wicked about him, Evan.'

'Realistic,' Evan shrugged. 'He's got no guts, and that makes me want to kick him.'

Like Steve, Evan had an aggressive masculinity which had no time for weaker members of his own sex. He had a very straightforward attitude to life. He treated women with a mixture of flattering admiration and a kindly contempt. He saw them in their roles as very much a second sex—playthings, mothers, housewives. Evan viewed the female members of staff as wives in the making—waiting out a brief time in the office before going off to do their real job as some man's wife. The world, in Evan's view of it, was the arena designed for man, the battlefield on which men demonstrated their masculinity and strength. Jon came into neither category. As a man, in Evan's book, he was a failure, and he wasn't a woman, so poor Jon became, necessarily, an irritant.

Lisa shook her head wryly at him. 'You have a very narrow-minded idea of life, Evan.'

His heavy face wore affront for a moment. 'Me?' Evan was rarely self-aware. Perhaps that was why he and Anna got on so well. They were each of them, in their separate ways, aggressive, certain, very unself-conscious.

'You and Anna are a perfect match,' she said thoughtfully, and Evan's face lightened and warmed again.

'Thank you,' he said, and his gratitude was heart-felt.

When she glanced round again she saw Steve turning the full battery of his charm on to Magda, who was hypnotised, agog. Lisa watched them and wanted to walk over there and hit him.

Instead she deliberately went over to Jon, who was talking earnestly to one of the accountants. The man gratefully escaped and Jon looked at her dully.

'I'm sorry,' she said gently.

'Why didn't you tell me?' Jon asked her, his fair skin flushing. 'I must have made a big fool of myself.'

'Of course not,' she said quickly. 'Neither of us had any serious intentions, did we? I knew that. We always said we were just good friends.'

Jon's relief was visible. She saw that the only thing bothering him was a suspicion that she had made him look foolish. He glanced over her slender, sensuous body and away again with red ears. Jon had always been more alarmed than attracted by her looks. He was aware that he would meet up with stiff competition if he really tried to capture her attention and he had always merely used her to boost his own ego in the office. That was why he was annoyed now. He was afraid that as a weapon against Evan and the other men she might have rebounded on his own head.

'Can I get you another drink?' he asked, glancing at her empty glass.

'Thank you.' He vanished to get it and at once some of the other men swooped on to Lisa and bombarded her with questions and teasing comments about her secret marriage. Some of them had persistently tried to take her out in the past and a slight pique was showing as they made jokes about it. She saw that they had been sniping at Jon continually over the past few days. She had let him in for that, and she was angry with herself.

Perhaps once he was in New York, away from Anna's loving, smothering protection, Jon would begin to harden into having a personality of his own. Somewhere there would be a girl who would immediately spot what Anna described as Jon's 'perfect husband material' qualities and grab him. He was a born sacrifice, a victim looking for a captor, a stray dog looking for a home. Those gentle, yielding qualities of his needed someone stronger to whom he could yield.

Marriage should be a dovetailing, a joining which completed. Her eyes wandered to where she could see Steve's broad shoulders as he leaned on the wall and looked down smilingly at Magda.

Where did they dovetail, meet? In their marriage, she now saw, they had barely even begun to discover that. The sexual attraction which had dragged them together had dimmed everything else to an unmeaning shadow. Did they have anything else? Was that all there was between them—that fierce passionate necessity which flamed up between them whenever they were alone?

She and Steve barely came into contact during the party. They moved around the room in opposite directions like satellites and Lisa always knew where he was by the cluster of girls who seemed to hang on every word he said. Steve was putting on an act he did very well—mocking, teasing, flirting lightly. She recognised it because she was doing it herself, she thought wryly.

Maybe they did have something in common at that. Maybe that was what had drawn them together, the fact that both of them assumed masks in public which bore no resemblance to the human being underneath. We all need to wear masks, but we also all need to discard them. Some of us only do that when we are alone and no other eye can see the real self exposed. Others need to have at least one other human being who knows the face behind the mask. Perhaps that was what the institution of marriage was all about. A man can only expose his weakness to two people in his life if he is to retain his self-respect—his mother and his wife. And even that can be dangerous because it gives such power into the hands of those who know the truth. We rely on love to safeguard us from the dangers of exposure.

Was that why Steve had refused to say 'I love you' since they met again? He had said it to her once and she had seemed to betray that trust. Steve had abandoned his mask to show his love for her and she had wounded him.

At eleven, Steve appeared behind her and touched her elbow lightly. She turned and he said coolly: 'Time to go, I'm afraid.'

Evan and the others protested, but Steve merely smiled and shrugged. 'We do have a plane to catch tomorrow.'

The goodbyes were noisy and protracted. Jon made his brief, but Evan insisted on a last kiss and, being very much under the influence of all the drink he had consumed, he took his time, only releasing her reluctantly.

Steve didn't say a word, but the hand which guided her out to the lift afterwards was not a kind one. Lisa glanced at him and said flatly: 'Evan doesn't give twopence for anyone but Anna.'

Steve didn't answer. He pushed her into the lift and stood there with his eyes fixed on the wall, his face hard.

When they got back to the flat he stood watching her in their bedroom as she nervously removed her make-up. The blue eyes were cold and speculative.

He came over and unzipped her dress, sliding his arms round her body to cup her breasts, his eyes meeting hers in the mirror.

'Come to bed,' he muttered, and she knew that whatever he was thinking he had no intention of showing her.

He was keeping that mask firmly in place. Even when she lay in his arms moaning under his hungry caresses, Steve was holding back, hiding his feelings. But now more than ever, Lisa was convinced that once he had her back in the States that mask would come off, and she was afraid of what she was going to find beneath it.

CHAPTER TEN

IT shook Lisa when they arrived at the airport to discover that they were not booked on a flight to Los Angeles, as she had imagined, but to Miami. Steve had not breathed a word of his intention and in the first few moments at the airport she was too busy making sure their baggage went off safely to realise exactly what flight they were taking. When it dawned on her she looked at Steve with a whitening face and stricken eyes.

He met her glance coolly, his face unrevealing.

'Why?' she asked in a low, shaken voice.

'I thought we should have a holiday alone before we go back to Los Angeles,' he told her in a calm voice which gave nothing away.

She stood there, torn between fear and confusion, her hands twisting together. What was behind this? The week in Florida a year ago had been the lowest point of her life, a week in hell, a week she wanted only to forget. Yet he was taking her back there quite deliberately. Was he going to repeat what had happened before? Was that in his mind?

She glanced towards the distant exit across the echoing airport. Above them the polite saccharine voices came and went, giving out changes in flights, announcements of departures. People streamed like lemmings going and coming. Children cried, men yawned, women fidgeted as they waited or eavesdropped on other people's conversations.

It was all so ordinary and boring and Lisa stood in the middle of it and her body was poised for flight, her nerves stretched to screaming point as she contemplated what Steve might be planning for her.

She had suspected it. Now she felt her suspicions hardening into a cold certainty.

He watched her, those blue eyes guarded, the lids hiding whatever expression lay in them, his hard face cool and speculative, waiting for her to act.

Steve knew she wanted to run. Although he was just standing there he was as poised as she was, waiting for her to move because he wasn't going to let her get away. If she tried to walk off he would hold her. He knew she would be reluctant to cause a scene here in public. He had deliberately hidden his intention from her. He had got her here and now he was going to get her on that plane. She wasn't going to escape him again.

She prayed that their flight would be delayed, that she would have time to think of a way to escape, but fate was not on her side. Steve had left it to the last moment to arrive. They only had a short wait before their flight was called. Lisa walked beside him along the windowed corridors with their faceless, uniform menacing inhumanity and she was ice-cold from her head to her feet. Steve moved beside her, not touching her, but his intention clamped down on her like manacles and she was shivering as she avoided his eyes.

Of course, she could just balk, refuse to board the plane; run and hide somewhere, plead sudden illness —there were ways of avoiding the trap into which he was leading her.

But she went on walking beside him and she did none of them. Seated beside him in the plane she let him clip her seatbelt home, her eyes not quite meeting his, and listened to the voice of the captain as he went through the usual ritual phrases. She had a pile of magazines on her lap. She flipped through them, glancing at the bright advertisements, seeing none of them, reading none of the words.

She ate plastic food she did not taste, drank brandy with her coffee and wished that the alcohol could make some alteration to the ice-cold stiffness of her hands and feet.

Closing her eyes, she willed herself to sleep, but such optimism was pointless. Her brain rehearsed those days and nights over and over again. She could not go through that again! it would kill her.

Steve barely spoke to her. She got the impression that he was now merely waiting with taut impatience for the moment when he had her in the cottage in Florida and his long-awaited vengeance could begin again. When she did venture a glance at him she found his face absorbed, his eyes fixed in thought.

She looked out of the window and saw the layered sky moving slowly and almost undetectably below them so that the plane seemed not to move but to hang suspended in space.

That was how she felt—suspended and waiting like a man going to his death.

She was exhausted and drained when they finally reached their destination. The long flight had seemed endless, yet it had also gone too fast, so that she had begun at the end to pray that they would slow down, be delayed, even crash. The prospect of what was waiting for her was so grim that she would have welcomed death as an alternative.

Steve had a car waiting for them. He drove them himself, his manner still coolly abstracted, and Lisa sat beside him and averted her eyes from the all too familiar, unforgotten landscape. The sound and sight of the sea did not bring the excited enjoyment it had once brought her when they got here. Steve had destroyed all that for her. Florida to her would always mean misery from now on, and no doubt Steve meant to make sure that the misery was even deeper and more destructive.

Their cottage was really far too large to justify the name, but it had amused them to retain it since guests always exclaimed in amusement when they saw the large white villa in its secluded gardens from which one could easily walk to the beach. The previous owners had called it White Cottage and Steve and Lisa had kept the name. During the first year of their marriage they had spent most of their leisure time here: long sunny days and enjoyable nights which had left a magic radiance around the place whenever she thought of it. That radiance had smashed, as she had been smashed, into a thousand glittering fragments.

Steve garaged the car while she went into the cottage and walked around it, shuddering at the memories it evoked. She went into the kitchen and found it spotless and empty. It was cared for and cleaned by a retired couple who lived half a mile away, but neither of them were here now.

She had made coffee when Steve joined her. He lounged in the pleasant room, eyeing her. 'Hungry?' she asked him politely.

'Yes,' he said in a voice which did not need any explanation.

Her hands shook. 'I've made some coffee,' she said quite unnecessarily, since the odour of the coffee permeated the air.

'What's the matter, Lisa?' Steve had mockery in his voice. 'You're very quiet.'

'I'm tired,' she said as coolly as she could.

'Too tired?' he asked softly.

She offered him his cup of coffee. 'I'll drink mine in the bathroom,' she muttered. 'I think I'll take a shower and then get some sleep. I'm suffering from jet-lag.'

'Oh, is that what it is?' he asked drily.

She went to her bedroom and stood still in the doorway, staring in shock and horror at what she saw.

For a long moment she just trembled, the cup in her hand shaking and sending hot coffee splashing over her wrist. A silent scream formed itself in her head.

Around the room were pinned row after row of glossy black-and-white blow-ups of herself, all identical, all horribly familiar. It was the famous photograph which had really started her climb to the top, the picture Denny had taken of her in white lingerie, her body deliberately posed to give the impression of an intense sexuality.

Lisa stared at them with eyes which were dilated with pain and terror.

Her own face stared back at her like an image in a nightmare, mocking her, the smouldering, alluring eyes filled with malicious laughter.

It isn't me, she thought. It never was. Denny imposed that on me and I let him, but it was never my real self. That image had haunted her ever since, though. She had been possessed by it, forced into appearing to be the sexual fantasy which Denny had created out of his own head and the raw material of her looks.

Denny had attempted to possess that fantasy in the end because he had been driven mad by the phantom he had raised. He had never even known the woman beneath that glossy mask.

Her hand shook even more violently and the cup clattered to the floor, spilling coffee over the white carpet and across her feet.

She turned and ran in manic flight along the passage and out through the darkened sunroom into the cool night air. Tearing through the garden, she received an impression of fragrance and shadows, the rising moon patterning the night in chequered black and white, the sound of the ocean growing louder as she drew nearer.

She kicked off her coffee-stained shoes and ran

over the pale sands staring at the ocean. Boundless, permanently in motion, it stretched milkily under the moon, the crystal scales of light trapped on its surface and flung back to the arching sky. Lisa stood there and breathed in the salt air, listened to the breathing of the waves. 'What am I going to do?' she cried out, but she cried into a silence which gave no answer.

She was stripped bare of everything but fear, groping for some assurance from the earth, the sky, the sea, and getting nothing from them but the reminder of their own existence. Human beings sank to nothing in the vast certainties of the universe. Her loneliness and fear were merely intensified by the great emptiness of the water, the ocean stretching to the furthermost limits of the human eye.

Steve was in the cottage waiting for her and when she went back there the long-drawn-out anguish would begin. She did not have to go back. She could walk away and keep walking along this empty silvered sand into the void which waited for her, because if she walked away from Steve life would be a void. Whatever he did to her, she needed him, needed his presence to assuage the loneliness she had never recognised until now with that emptiness of sea and sky in front of her, forcing her to admit her own humanity and isolation. She stood there, shivering with the tremors of fear and recoil, feeling the hot pulse beating at her throat and wrists beneath all that, because, however he hurt her, Steve brought her to life too.

Denny had locked her inside an image which had

never borne any resemblance to her inner self, but Steve had freed her from it. He had pierced the mask and released her. That was why he had married her. The girl with sexy alluring eyes, the girl whose sensuous body promised such delight, had not been the girl Steve married. He had married Lisa for what was beneath her mask, and when he thought she had been deceiving him, that the mask was a true reflection after all, Steve had reacted with savagery and pain.

Time gives back recurring dreams and she was falling into one now, helpless, resigned, because as she watched the ocean sliding up on to the white sand she knew she was going back to what waited for her. In the deep green caverns of the mind among the weeds and stones which have no meaning, time's contract was scaled, the dreams resolved their theme. If she was to leap past the false image she had to go back to him.

She turned slowly, and he stood there watching her, a dark figure in the shadows and moonlight. She could not guess how long he had stood there and his face told her nothing of what he was thinking.

Slowly she walked towards him and the moon slid with butterfinger lightness over her, lifting her face into the light and dropping it again, shifting the white features to give them partial illumination.

She felt that Steve was a total stranger; she had never known him. Together they walked back into the cottage and he followed her into her bedroom. She did not look at the photographs again, her head bent.

Steve walked round and stripped them down with a fierce gesture, ripped them across and flung them to the floor. 'I'd forgotten they were there,' he said, staring at her. 'I spent the last year looking at them, but I'd forgotten they were still there, Lisa.'

She was tracing the pale coffee stains which had sunk into the carpet. 'We'll have to have the carpet cleaned,' she said in the tones of a polite visitor. 'I'm sorry.'

He came towards her and she did not flinch or back away. Steve put his arms round her and held her tightly against him, one hand moving among her hair, his fingers gently caressing.

'You looked lonely out there by the sea,' he said huskily.

She nodded and pushed her face into his shoulder, nuzzling his warm flesh for human comfort. Her arms went round his waist and she held him, feeling the tension of the muscles in his long back.

'I love you,' he said with his lips at her forehead. 'I love you, Lisa.'

She clutched him tighter and the tears welled up into her eyes. They poured out into his shirt and he gave a groan. 'Don't,' he said. 'Don't, darling.'

'Why did you bring me here? Why here?' she asked in shaking tones. 'How could you?'

'We have to wipe it out, darling, don't you see that? I wanted it to be here that I told you I loved you again. I wanted us to cover those terrible memories with new ones. It's the only way. If we went back to Los Angeles it wouldn't be the same. It had to be here. I'd forgotten I'd pinned those damned pictures round your room. When you didn't come back I went to find you and there was your cup and coffee all over the carpet and those pictures on the wall. I was terrified.' He tilted her head and framed it between his hands. She felt the faint tremor in his fingers, she saw the darkness in his eyes. 'I couldn't bear to lose you again,' Steve muttered hoarsely. 'You make me real.'

It was what she had faced out there on the empty beach. They needed each other because somehow together they became real. Lisa had never felt real because at such an early age Denny had imposed that image on her. Steve had had an image imposed on him, too, although she had never realised it until now. His family had forced him into the mould prepared for him.

Steve had inherited wealth and power and been taught how to use it, but under that had been another man, although even now she was not sure exactly what Steve was, only that something in herself reached out to him and got back an answer.

'We've got to learn to live together again,' Steve said.

Lisa was trembling with relief and an unbelievable sensation of happiness. He felt the shaking in her body and looked at her with anxiety, the blue eyes probing her face.

'Lisa?'

She wound her arms around his neck and offered him her mouth, her eyes closed.

His mouth came down in burning possession, wringing every ounce of response from her, his hands stroking down her body with an eagerness he did not disguise and which made her flame into receptive excitement.

He lifted her into his arms and carried her to the bed. She clung, her arms round his neck, her lips swollen and heated from the long kiss. The passion they had exchanged during the past days had been a prelude to the unleashed violence with which they made love now. It had been on this bed that Steve had set out to destroy her self-respect, and now they cleansed it with the fiery sweetness of their present lovemaking.

Afterwards they lay on the bed, her head on his shoulder, the cool night wind blowing through the room from the open window, and talked in hushed and sleepy voices.

'I'd like to have a baby,' she murmured, her lips on his warm skin.

'No career?' he asked, smiling.

'No,' she said. 'I envied Anna. She had it all—Evan and her boys and then the new baby. She was mad, risking it all for Jon.'

'You don't have to give up your career, Lisa,' Steve said quietly. 'Don't do it to please me.'

'I'm not, I'm pleasing myself. It was all a mistake —I got caught up in it, but I never actively wanted it. I think perhaps I never got the chance to be myself.' She had been like someone standing idly on a beach who gets carried away by a great wave and never knows what would have happened to them if fate had not struck them down like that. If she had never met Denny that day she might have become a secre-

tary or a receptionist, but she would never have
hankered for the life of a top class photographic
model because such an ambition had never entered
her head.

Steve gave a faint sigh and she turned her head to
look at him through the moonlit darkness. 'Do you
disagree?' she asked.

He smiled drily at her. 'I wanted you to make up
your own mind, but I won't pretend I'm not delighted. I want you at home, Lisa. I want a wife and
children. We'll have holidays here in the cottage and
I'll teach the children to swim and surf and maybe
fish.'

Steve had always liked outdoor sports. He was a
man who liked the sun and the sea and physical ac-
tivity. All his reactions were physical ones—that was
the basis of their sexual rapport. Their bodies were
drawn to each other, but their minds had never had
the chance to learn the secrets each was hiding.

He presented his colleagues and clients with a picture of a smooth, sophisticated man who knew his
way around the world in which he was forced to
operate, but looking back all Lisa could remember
of their time together were simple pleasures, needing
neither money nor expertise; the delight of spending
hours in the sun beside the ocean, basking like children in the sun or diving in and out of the rolling
waves. Steve had always preferred an evening spent
at home with her in Los Angeles to the noisy gaiety
of a party or a night at some expensive night-spot.
She had never connected all these things because she
had not been sufficiently self-aware to realise what

she was learning about him. When they did go out together Steve was always eager to get home, to be
alone with her. In company she had often found him
watching her with a light in those blue eyes which
told her what was in his mind. The sexual pleasure
they gave each other had not been the only reason
why Steve grew bored with night-clubs and parties.
He might be able to present a convincing image of
sophistication, but his real nature inclined him to be
happier in his own home with one of his huge collection of jazz recordings playing, or driving with her on
a warm summer evening, just enjoying the sensation
of speed and the wind in his black hair. He had liked
to have her cook for him, amused to watch her briskly
performing the little tasks of dicing vegetables or
rolling out pastry. Steve's pleasures had all been
simple and they had all been laid open to her from the
start. It had been her own blindness that did not make
the connections and work out what sort of man she
had married.

Steve had probably always wanted her to give up her
career and devote herself to being his wife and the
mother of his children, but he had respected her integ-
rity as a human being enough to leave her free to make
the choice herself, no doubt believing that sooner or
later she would tire of her career and choose to give it
up.

Her earlier terror had receded to the point where she
no longer even remembered it. She lay happily in his
arms and was aware of a sensation of belonging, of security. From the start Steve had offered her that, but
she had not realised it.

'I have my dreams too,' Steve murmured huskily.

She turned her cheek to look at his inverted face, smiling at him. 'Do you? Tell me.'

'You,' he whispered, his lips on her cloudy hair.

She smiled, her mouth brushing his shoulder. 'Mmm, and what else, darling?'

'You,' he said in a voice which stripped away the masks from both of them for ever.

Lisa lifted her head. His face was alight with moonlight and passion, the blue eyes glittering and intent. Lisa felt her heart stop, then start again with a hammering speed which shook her whole body.

'You,' Steve said again, laying bare for her his own loneliness and need and the stark reality of their involvement.

'Darling,' she muttered with lips that trembled.

He found her mouth with a hunger which their earlier lovemaking had done nothing to assuage. It had never been enough—the urgent passion with which their bodies clung had been unable to feed the inner hunger. They had always been left unsated, famished, still craving for some satisfaction they never managed to reach.

The flesh could not dissolve between them, the barrier of their own separate selves impassable, and still they kissed, their arms around each other, admitting silently the need to be completed and made whole. Lisa felt the flowering of the future in her veins and hope was no longer a distant stranger, but a real and present promise.

Harlequin understands

Love...

and the way you feel about it...

That's why women all over the world read

Harlequin Romances

Beautiful novels with that special blend
of Harlequin magic...the thrill
of exotic places, the appeal of warmly
human characters, the tenderness
and sparkle of first love.

Enjoy six brand-new novels every month—
contemporary romances about women
like you...for women like you!

Available at your favorite bookstore or through
Harlequin Reader Service

In U.S.A.
MPO Box 707
Niagara Falls,
NY 14302

In Canada
649 Ontario St.
Stratford,
Ontario N5A 6W2

Harlequin Presents...

The books that let you escape
into the wonderful world of romance!
Trips to exotic places...interesting
plots...meeting memorable people...
the excitement of love....These are
integral parts of Harlequin Presents—
the heartwarming novels read by
women everywhere.

Many early issues are now available.
Choose from this great selection!

Choose from this great selection of exciting Harlequin Presents editions

Relive a great romance... with Harlequin Presents

Complete and mail this coupon today!

Harlequin Reader Service

Please send me the following Harlequin Presents novels. I am enclosing my check or money order for $1.50 for each novel ordered, plus 59¢ to cover postage and handling.

☐ 192	☐ 201	☐ 210
☐ 193	☐ 202	☐ 211
☐ 194	☐ 203	☐ 212
☐ 195	☐ 204	☐ 213
☐ 197	☐ 205	☐ 214
☐ 198	☐ 206	☐ 215
☐ 199	☐ 207	☐ 216
☐ 200	☐ 208	☐ 217

Number of novels checked @ $1.50 each =	$_____
N.Y. and Ariz. residents add appropriate sales tax.	$_____
Postage and handling	$_____.59
TOTAL	$_____

I enclose _____
(Please send check or money order. We cannot be responsible for cash sent through the mail.)

Prices subject to change without notice.

NAME _____
(Please Print)

ADDRESS _____

CITY _____

STATE/PROV. _____

ZIP/POSTAL CODE _____

Offer expires March 31, 1981   101563170